Angel By My Side

GRACE'S STORY

Other *Avon Camelot Books in the*
ANGEL BY MY SIDE *Trilogy by*
Erin Flanagan

AMELIA'S STORY
LILY'S STORY

Angel By My Side

GRACE'S STORY

ERIN FLANAGAN

AN AVON CAMELOT BOOK

ANGEL BY MY SIDE: GRACE'S STORY is an original publication of Avon Books. This work has never before appeared in book form.

AVON BOOKS
A division of
The Hearst Corporation
1350 Avenue of the Americas
New York, New York 10019

Copyright © 1995 by Erin Flanagan
Published by arrangement with the author
Library of Congress Catalog Card Number: 95-94496
ISBN: 0-380-78255-3
RL: 4.8

First Avon Camelot Printing: December 1995

CAMELOT TRADEMARK REG. U.S. PAT. OFF. AND IN OTHER COUNTRIES, MARCA REGISTRADA, HECHO EN U.S.A.

Printed in the U.S.A.

OPM 10 9 8 7 6 5 4 3 2 1

To A.A.B.
My S.S.L.

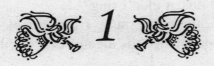

1

"I think you should go to the Rose Parade tomorrow." Lily, my guardian angel, crossed her arms and smiled.

"It's too crowded," I said with a shake of my head, "and besides, Mom won't let me go alone." I turned my attention back to the pot of caramel corn I was stirring.

"Amelia, don't make me cajole you." Lily appeared at my elbow. "We angels have ways of making you do our bidding."

The corners of my mouth turned up in response to her teasing. "Oh yeah? What will you do? Flutter at me?"

"Noooo. I won't have to. You'll see." She peered over my shoulder into the pot. "What on earth *is* that stuff? You don't intend to ingest it, do you?"

"It's caramel corn. And it's yummy. We have it every

New Year's Eve. You want some? It's done.'' I pulled the wooden spoon out of the goo and offered it to her. "Taste."

"No, and don't you eat it either."

"Why not? I love it."

"Because you are wanted on the phone."

"No I'm not, it didn't ring."

Just then, the phone rang. I shot a look in Lily's direction. "Something tells me this is about that dumb old parade."

"What makes you say that?" she asked with a mischievous smile.

"Amelia!" screeched my younger sister, Kate, "Flinkman on the phone!"

"Okay, okay, they can hear you in China!" I grabbed the phone and turned the television down with the remote. "Hello?"

"Happy New Year!"

"Happy to you, too, Richard. What are you doing?"

"Hanging out with my parents, what else? We do a jigsaw puzzle every New Year's Eve. Keeps me off the streets. What's cookin' over there?"

I laughed at my sort-of, semi-boyfriend. "We're having caramel corn and watching New Year's Rockin' Eve from Times Square."

"The excitement is almost more than we can bear, right?"

"Yeah. But what else is there to do? Besides, my parents went to a party, so I have to watch Kate.''

"You don't have to watch me!" she shouted indignantly from her burrow in the beanbag chair. "I'm in the fourth grade! I can watch myself do whatever I'm going to do!"

"Boy, her volume is amazing! It seems we both have puzzles to work on tonight," Richard said with a chuckle. "But how about if we go to the Rose Parade in the morning?"

I sighed, and glanced at Lily who was hovering near the front window. She winked at me.

An angel with attitude, I thought as I gave up and accepted my fate. "Okay. I've never been. I guess I should see it at least once."

"That's the spirit!"

"You can say that again!" I said as I watched Lily clap her hands with glee.

"That's the spirit!"

"Okay, Rich, okay. What's the parade plan?"

"The plan is to get up and out at five and buzz over to Pasadena, courtesy of my mom and the Flinkmobile. Lots of people camp out all night to get the best spots, but that is off-limits until I'm sixteen, so we'll have to push up in front of some old people in lounge chairs to get a good view."

"We can't do that!"

"Sure we can. We'll keep them company and protect them from the riffraff.''

"They'll think we're the riffraff!"

"Us! Are you kidding? We're about as riffraffy as Nancy Drew and Ned Nickerson."

I laughed. "Okay, okay. We'll find a spot nice and early. Is it all right if Kate comes? She's never seen it either."

Kate sprang from her beans and jumped around in front of me. "Yeah! Can I come, can I come?"

I motioned at her to stop jumping.

"Sure, bring the little Katerator. My mom can help us keep track of her. I mean, it's not like this is a real date or anything."

"Of course not," I agreed. "We're just pals."

"Yeah. 'Pals 'R Us.' We'll pick you up at the crack, okay?"

"Okay. We'll be ready!" I hung up and watched the television screen as the big ball in Times Square dropped slowly toward earth. It always made me a little sad for some reason. Everything from the past year sunk with that ball.

Kate tugged me into the new year. "Do I get to go with you?"

I nodded.

"Yippee!" She danced around the room and landed back in front of me. "Where do I get to go?"

I shook my head and smiled. "Come on, let's go eat our caramel corn. I'll tell you then."

We settled at the kitchen table and I explained the plan.

"This will be so much gobs of fun! I've only seen the parade on TV." Kate licked caramel from her fingers. "Are you excited, Amelia?"

"Sure."

"Maybe you are, but you seem sad around the edges."

"Oh, I don't know." I leaned back and listened to the sounds of revelers in our neighborhood and on TV. "Last year is gone. My very best friend, Shura, is gone. I finished the book about ugly ducklings. Endings are sad to me."

"But Mommy and Mr. C. got married this past year, and we got a new house, and I've almost got them talked into getting a puppy, and you might get to be in the school play and we're going to the parade and . . ."

"I know, I know. But listen to that song they're singing on television. That 'Auld Lang Syne' song . . ."

She crinkled her nose. "I don't get that song. They made us sing it at school during music. The words are goofy."

"They're just old fashioned words."

"They're still goofy. What do they mean?"

"I'm not sure exactly, but I think . . ." I felt Lily's hand touch my forehead and the familiar tingle went up my spine. "I think it means we should try to remember people and things from our past, so that they never really die."

"That's nice. They should sing it that way, so people get it easier."

"Maybe it's like a hard puzzle," I mused. "Maybe

5

we're supposed to have to figure some stuff out for ourselves.''

"Then what about that part they just sang? *We'll take
it up with kindness, then.* What's that?''

"I think it's, *take a cup of kindness yet, for days of
auld lang syne.*''

"Huh?''

"It means we should drink from the cup of kindness
and then kindness will be in us. And the past will be in
us too.''

"You're smart, Amelia,'' said Kate. "I'm glad I'm
your little sister.''

"And I am honored to be your angel,'' whispered Lily
into my left ear.

Just then Mom and our new dad came home. We tum-
bled over each other to give hugs and tell about our parade plans.

"It sure is dark and cold in the morning.'' Kate's
words came out in cool little puffs and hung in the air
outside our house. "This is the darkest dark I've ever
seen.''

"The dark isn't so bad,'' said Dad as he gathered us
closer to him. "It just has a bad reputation.''

"Daddy, isn't it scary to be blind?''

Mr. C. (I still had to remind myself to call him
"Dad'') smiled and shook his head. "No, Katie, it isn't
scary. I'm too busy paying attention to other things to
be scared.''

"Like what?"

"Like the sound of my footsteps as they bounce back at me from the buildings and trees, like the feel of shade and of light, like the tone of a voice, like the touch of a hand. I can smell excitement in the air when the wind is right."

"You see more than me!" she replied with surprise.

"In some ways, I do. Like right now, I know a car is coming. Hear it?"

Kate strained forward. "I'm squinting my ears, but I don't hear it."

We laughed and stood closer together.

"Here they come now." I squeezed Dad's hand and grabbed Kate by hers. "See ya, Dad!"

"See ya!" he replied with a wave.

We climbed into the Flink family station wagon and greeted our hosts. We drove through silently eerie streets until we hit the far end of Colorado Boulevard in Pasadena.

"Man, look at all these people. Maybe we better park and walk, Mom," said Richard.

"Yes. It will probably be more expedient that way." She locked the car doors and admonished us to stay together. "I'll never find you if we get separated in this sea of humanity!"

"I love how you talk, Mrs. Flink," said Kate, slipping her hand into the older woman's. "Being an English teacher must be fun."

Richard laughed and fell into step with me. "Kate has

7

made a friend for life now. Mom will probably have her majoring in English lit before the parade is over!''

''Could be, although last I heard, Kate wanted to go to clown college in Florida and work for either the circus or McDonald's.''

''That would be good training to teach, me thinks!'' he replied.

I laughed. ''Come on, Shakespeare. Let's hurry and find a spot. The sun's coming up.''

''But look, the morn in russet mantle clad, walks o'er the dew of yon high eastward hill!''

''What?'' Kate turned and gawked at Richard.

''He said the sun's coming up,'' I said.

Mrs. Flink laughed. ''That's my boy!''

The sun peeped at us over the San Gabriel Mountains as we picked our way carefully over the sleeping bags, mattresses, camping stoves, and lounge chairs of the diehard parade lovers who had been camped out since yesterday morning.

''Let's go to Orange Grove Boulevard,'' suggested Richard. ''We can sit near the television booths. They have a great view.''

''Can we sit in those grandstands?'' asked Kate as we neared the beginning of the parade route.

''No way, kid. Those cost big bucks and you have to get tickets in advance.'' Richard tweaked her disappointed chin.

''Wow! I can't believe this,'' I said as I looked

around. "There must me a zillion people here. They look like wall-to-wall carpeting."

"One million, two hundred and thirteen," whispered Lily, whom I could hear and then see just behind my left shoulder. "And the thirteenth person is Grace Slick Jamison."

I cringed and looked around. There she was: "Slick" Jamison, one of the wild girls from my junior high. A girl whose acquaintance I had carefully not made. Why was Lily always bringing her up?

"This is a miracle!" said Mrs. Flink. "It's as if this spot was just waiting for us! And right down front, too!"

Richard, Kate, and Mrs. Flink staked their claim to the prime stretch of curb that appeared before us. I hung back to talk to Lily.

"Thanks a bunch," I muttered under my breath to her.

"You're so welcome," she whispered sweetly. "Now you'll be just a few feet from Slick and her friends."

"Will wonders never cease?" I remarked.

"I certainly hope not," she sang as she fluttered off in the direction of Slick.

I sighed and accepted my next angelic encounter. "I'll be right back, you guys. I have to go and say 'hi' to someone."

They waved me off with a smile and an assurance that they would save my place.

I stood warily on the fringes of Slick's crowd and watched her.

Her laugh was dry and brittle, like last year's Christmas candy. She had dyed her hair (again) over the school break, and it was a shade not found in nature's palette of hair colors, sort of a dark maroon.

A nose ring had been added to her left nostril and I guessed that a tattoo was not far behind. Or maybe it already was behind.

She liked to wear tee shirts with messages on them. Today's said UP YOURS.

I guess I was staring, because Slick sidled over to me and said, "Take a picture, why don't you? It lasts longer."

"Oh, um, sorry."

"Right." She laughed, took a drag on her cigarette, and blew the smoke at me.

A dragon sprang to mind.

I turned away and headed for my comfy piece of curb. Lily appeared in front of me, a question mark on her lovely face.

"Forget it," I said, "No way. She is a freak of nature. And she's dangerous. I'm not doing it. Get somebody else."

Lily put her arm around me. "You're afraid."

"You've got that right!"

"Well, so is she."

"Hah!" People were nudging each other and staring at me, so I lowered my voice and slipped into an empty doorway. "Why should she be afraid?"

10

"That's what you need to find out, my dear." Lily put an imaginary cup to her lips.

I sighed with exasperation. "Okay, okay, I'll drink a cup of kindness. But it's only for you."

"That's what you think."

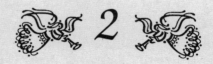

2

"I always thought you'd be able to smell the flowers on the floats as they went by," observed Mrs. Flink as the parade began. "But I don't smell a single one, which is odd, considering that there must be millions of them along this parade route."

Richard leaned forward from the curb and sniffed. "You're right, Mom, not a whiff. All you can smell is the exhaust from the floats." He sniffed again. "And I think I smell coffee and somebody grilling hot dogs."

"How come it's called the Rose Parade?" asked Kate. "There's more flowers than just roses. Look, there are daffodils, and violets, and tulips, and crysnathimoms, and lotsa flowers I've never even met."

"Ask Miss Hollywood History over there," said Richard, pointing at me. "She'll know a bunch of obscure stuff."

I laughed and grabbed my cold, knocking knees. "Actually, I just read in the *L.A. Times* that the parade started in 1890 when the townspeople draped garlands of roses over their horse-and-buggy carriages and old carts to celebrate what good weather we have in Southern California, even in winter."

"Excuse me for listening in," said an old lady who was sitting next to me, "but what does that have to do with football? That Rose Bowl game seems more important than the parade nowadays." She sipped something from a 7-Eleven Big Gulp cup and adjusted her lounge chair.

"Well, Ma'am, I read that originally, they had a 'Battle of the Flowers' where they put on a real Roman chariot race, along with ostrich races. That got too dangerous, so they started the football game back in 1916."

She nodded and shook the ice around in her cup. "Ahhh. I guess they figured football was safer than galloping ostriches, huh?"

"Less clean-up!" quipped Richard.

I smiled, shook my head, and continued, "I guess so. At least safer than 1913, that was the year they raced camels and elephants . . ." Something hit me in the back of the head and I turned abruptly.

People all around me were turning and feeling the backs of their heads.

I spotted Lily hovering and pointing at something. It

was Slick and her friends, throwing warmed, gooey marshmallows into the crowd and laughing hysterically.

I sighed and rolled my eyes.

The old woman next to me stood up and leaned on her cane. "You hooligans get out of here! You make it bad for all of us!" She sat down and grumbled, "Imagine having nothing better to do than harass other people!"

Slick and her friends disappeared into the crowds just as two police officers hurried over.

How was nice little old me supposed to deal with someone who had the police on her trail?

Lily appeared next to me and whispered, "Don't worry. You'll know what to do when the moment is upon you."

I nodded uncertainly. All I could do was hope.

But it sure looked hopeless.

Suddenly Kate jumped up and darned near ran right into the parade route. Richard grabbed the back of her sweatshirt just in time. She kept running as he held her, like a cartoon character.

"Kate! Get back here!" I jumped up and pulled her down on the curb next to me. "What in the heck are you doing? You could get scrunched out there under those monster floats!"

"Look! Look! Aren't they beautiful?" She pointed and gazed up at the float just crossing in front of us.

Richard and I looked at each other and back at the mountain of moving flowers and white, waving gloves.

"What's the big deal, Katerator?" he asked. "It's just the float with the flowery queen, or posy princess, or whatever she's called. Along with her buds, or sprouts, or elves, or whatever they're called."

Kate put her hands on her hips and thrust her chin at him. "You are ignore-ant, Richard. That is the Rose *Queen* and her official *Court*! They're almost the most important thing in the whole parade!"

"It's ignorant," he corrected, trying to hide a smile. "And I think 'buds' is better than 'court' any day."

"You're just a dumb boy, so you wouldn't know anything anyway."

"Kate, don't call names," I said.

"Well, he doesn't know!" she insisted. "I'd love to be up there on that float, just like her. She gets to wear a beautiful dress, and those long gloves, and she gets to wave to us, and everybody who is watching on television sees her . . ." She paused for air. "*And* she gets to wear that crown made of real jewels!"

I could hardly believe my ears. I had spent the past months putting together a book about girls who feel ugly and how important it is to be more than just our faces, and here was my little sister going ga-ga over a beauty queen!

"Are you crazy!" I grabbed her hand and made her look at me. "Wouldn't you rather be doing something fun in the parade instead of sitting on your tuffet and waving?"

"How do you know it's not fun to be the prettiest and

15

to wear a gown and a crown and wave? Huh? How do you know?''

"I don't." And it was true. I didn't know for sure. How could I? I would never be the gown, crown, waving kind of girl.

The difference was, I no longer wanted to be. The price was too high.

"Listen, Katerator," said Richard. "Those girls are like decorations or something. They're not much different than the flowers. Wouldn't you rather be one of the clowns or one of the people who gets to *do* something, instead of *ride* on something?''

"No. I want to be the Rose Queen, and I don't care what you guys say.''

Mrs. Flink interrupted us. "Now, children, let's not fuss. Kate is a little girl and little girls sometimes want to be princesses and such. It's just a stage.''

"I'm not a stage and I want to be *queen*.'' Kate shoved her hands into her sweatshirt pockets.

"Excuse me, dear, I meant to say queen.'' Mrs. Flink winked at us and put her arm around Kate. "Why don't you come with me to the food court, and we'll bring back hot chocolate for everyone.''

"Okay,'' grumbled Kate, "but I still want to be queen.'' She took Mrs. Flink's hand and I watched as her ponytail seemed to trot behind her.

"Man, what got into her?'' Richard scratched his head and looked at me.

"Don't ask me. I thought after I wrote *Swan Songs*,

she would get the idea that there's more to life than looks."

"Maybe it's like my dad says."

"What's that?"

"Well, he says that lessons are learned from experience, not observation."

"You mean, like Kate has to feel it before she can know it?"

"Yeah, like that."

"I guess so. But I wish she'd just take my word for it."

"Nah. She has to take her own word for it."

I laughed. "And right now, that word is *Queen*."

"Young lady, excuse me. Young lady? I have another parade question for you." The old lady next to us tugged at my sleeve.

"Sure. I'll give it a try."

"You mentioned that one year they had camel and elephant races, and I got to wondering who won that race?"

"The elephants won."

She nodded knowingly. "Yes. Elephants usually do, don't they?"

"I guess they just crush the competition," said Richard.

The old lady laughed so hard she nearly fell out of her chair. "What a pleasure it is to meet such nice young people! Not like those street urchins that were throwing things earlier."

I thought of Slick and my promise to help her. I hoped that street urchins weren't like elephants.

Just then, Kate ran up to us holding a cardboard tray of sloshing hot chocolate. Mrs. Flink was hurrying to keep up.

"Guess what? Guess what?" asked Kate breathlessly.

"What?" asked Richard, me, and the old lady.

"I was standing there, helping Mrs. Flink, and telling her about being queen, when I saw a sign in a store window and I went in and got one! It was like magic that it happened!"

We exchanged puzzled glances.

"What Kate means," explained Mrs. Flink, "is that she saw an advertisement in a shop window for a local beauty pageant. The proprietor of the store had applications, and he gave one to her." She shrugged at us over Kate's head.

Kate thrust the paper into my hands.

I read:

ENTER! ENTER!
The Prestigious
Miss Young Sunny California Beauty Pageant!
Girls Aged 4-17
February 14—Marriott Grand Ballroom
Beauty and poise judged by an important panel!
Application (signed by parents) due at
Preliminary pageant held January 24 at 1 P.M.

I looked at Kate. She was smiling like a beauty contestant.

A big, happy sun smiled up at me, too, from the application.

I swallowed my reservations, smiled at my little sister, and hoped Mom wouldn't sign it.

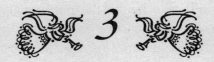

3

"**I** can't believe you're going to let her do this," I said as I slapped peanut butter onto a bagel and threw it into a plastic bag.

"Noel and I discussed it and decided we should let Kate see for herself what it's like." Mom handed me a drink box and I shoved it into my lunch sack.

"But, Mom, it's so . . . so . . . stinky!"

"Stinky? Aren't you the girl who used to watch the Miss America Pageant each and every year? You didn't think it was stinky then."

"I was just a kid!"

"Exactly. That's what your sister is, too. Just a kid. She thinks it will be like something out of a Disney movie. The best way to learn it isn't, is by seeing it first

20

hand.'' She poured herself more coffee and leaned against the sink.

''I guess. But I'd be worried that she'll love it and become a little beauty pageant maniac.'' I gathered up my books and piled them into my backpack.

''Okay, Amelia, I know you're worried, so I was wondering if you'd take her to the preliminary pageant for me. You know, keep an eye on her and make sure this thing is on the up and up. I have a staff meeting that day at the hospital that I absolutely cannot miss.''

''Sure, I'll take her!'' I had to admit, I was kind of curious about the whole thing.

''Good. That will be such a help.'' She patted my behind. ''Have a good day at school. I know the first day after the vacation is always a bit, ah . . . stinky.''

''The perfect word for certain things!'' I said with a laugh.

Mom patted her tummy. ''Yes. It describes how I'm feeling this morning as well.''

''Are you sick, Mom?'' I felt her forehead as she had so often felt mine. ''You're not hot.''

''No, I don't think I'm sick. It's probably just the holiday goodies coming back to haunt me. I knew I shouldn't eat that caramel corn.'' She smiled and rinsed out her coffee cup. ''Don't worry. I'm fine. You have a good day, and let me know how the play tryouts go this afternoon.''

''I will. Kiss Mr., ah, kiss Dad for me. I've got to run to catch the bus.''

21

"Be careful! Bye!"

I made it to the bus stop just in time.

In fact, Lily had to hold the doors for me. The bus driver couldn't figure out why they wouldn't close!

We settled into a far back seat of the almost empty public bus. The few people on board were wearing portable stereo headphones, so we could talk.

"You don't need to worry about Kate, you know," Lily said. "Cyril is always with her, even though she doesn't mention him anymore. He'll keep an eye on things."

"I know, Lily, but I want to keep an eye on things, too."

"Good. You should help him. We angels have been working a lot of overtime lately." She patted my hand. "I just wanted to remind you that no one is ever completely alone."

"Even Slick Jamison?"

"Of course. Her too. She has an angel, but she blocks her out. She can see you though, so she won't be able to block you out."

"I'm not so sure about that."

Lily smiled. "I'm sure enough for both of us."

"Great. I still don't see how I can even get near her. She's a year older than me, so we have no classes together. I don't have a clue where she eats lunch. Probably in some hidden, smoky corner of the school. I don't know where she lives, and I don't want to go to the streets where she hangs out."

22

"Sounds as if you have put a lot of energy into figuring out how this puzzle won't work." Lily opened her hand and a white butterfly appeared.

I gazed at it. Its crystalline wings opened and closed delicately.

"People are like this," whispered Lily. "Their spirits so pure and fragile. But nowadays they are so unhappy, and they have forgotten that, deep inside, they know how to fly." She raised her hand and the butterfly flew out the open window.

I looked into Lily's loving blue eyes.

"I see," I said quietly. "And I'll try to remember."

"Of course you will, dear, gentle Amelia. You see me because you do remember."

The bus ground to a halt and I stepped out of Lily's world and into the world of school.

It was like stepping into a whirlpool. If you're not careful, it will suck you down.

All day long, as I went to class, showered in P.E. and ate lunch with my school friend, Luana, I thought about Slick and tried to come up with a plan. I couldn't think of a thing.

By the time I got to Honors English, I had put the Slick problem out of my mind. It was time to concentrate on Mr. Jacobs, my English teacher, and his plan to put on the play version of *The Diary of Anne Frank*.

He stopped me after class.

"Now, you'll be at the meeting of Drama Club today, won't you, Amelia? I'm counting on you to try out for

23

the lead." He scribbled some notes on the chalkboard and wiped the chalk dust onto his pants.

"I'll be there. This will be my first time to join a club in junior high. You guys meet in the auditorium, don't you?"

"Yes, and I'll have copies of the play for all of you to study for fifteen minutes or so. Then each of you will read a section out loud with scripts in hand. Next time I'll expect everyone to have memorized a speech from the play."

"Okay. I'll see you there!" I smiled and headed for my locker. I was kind of nervous about this whole play thing. Some of the kids in drama were two years older than me and it made me kind of antsy. Ninth graders had a way of looking at you that said, "What rock did you crawl out from under?"

Then they tried to step on you.

I was almost the first one at Drama Club.

Slick Jamison was already there when I walked in.

Lily smiled at me from up in the ropes and pulleys above the curtains. She was swinging on a rope and humming.

Slick sneered at me, and I wished I could join Lily up in the air.

"What are you doing here? You're not in drama!" Slick pulled up one thin leg and tightened the laces on her black military boots.

I couldn't tell if she was asking me or accusing me.

"Mr. Jacobs asked me to join. He says you guys are doing *The Diary of Anne Frank*, and he thinks I should try out." I set my stuff on a chair and tried to look . . . dramatic.

She sighed heavily, and took off her khaki army jacket. Her shirt said LIFE HAPPENS, THEN YOU STEP IN IT.

She saw me reading it and laughed. "Like it? My boyfriend gave it to me. I think it says it all, don't you?"

Lily stopped humming.

I swallowed. Should I agree to make her like me? But I didn't agree. I looked up. Lily looked down. Slick looked annoyed.

I cleared my throat. "No. I think it says what you think, not what is."

Lily started humming again.

I smiled at Slick. She glowered.

"Yeah. What do you know? You're just a Miss Priss."

"And you are . . . Miss Taken."

"Miss what? Oh, ha, ha. That's so funny, I could almost laugh. What a freak."

Just then, five or six kids came in followed by Mr. Jacobs. I breathed a sigh of relief. I knew Lily had said Slick was meant to be my friend, but I didn't even like being alone in the same room with her!

Some friendship this would be.

"Okay, okay, let's start passing out scripts," said Mr. Jacobs. "We'll wait ten minutes for the stragglers, then

25

each of you choose a piece of dialogue for the character you wish to portray.''

''There are more people than parts,'' said Slick. ''I only joined this stupid school club to get out of serving detention. I'm not gonna just sit around and stagnate, I might as well be *in* detention! What will the people who don't get a role get stuck doing?''

''Oh, have no fear, we'll need help with costumes, scenery, makeup, and selling tickets. I'll be sure everyone gets a job either behind the scenes or in front of them.'' Mr. Jacobs smiled and wished each of us good luck.

I flipped through the play and chose a small speech in the first act.

When my turn came, I was so nervous, it felt as if I had a mouth full of cotton. But I got through it.

''Fine, Amelia,'' said Mr. Jacobs, ''but, next time speak up. You need to project your voice to the back of the theater.''

I nodded and blushed.

Next was Slick. She was also reading for the part of Anne.

''Okay, Grace. Good job,'' said Mr. Jacobs when she had finished. ''Remember though, Anne is not angry. She is accepting of what life has handed her. What she wants is to understand why.''

Slick looked confused. ''But, wouldn't she be, like, really pissed at what the Nazis were doing to her?''

"I don't think so. Being 'really pissed' wouldn't have helped her, would it?"

"Couldn't hurt!" said Slick.

Everyone laughed.

I raised my hand.

"Yes, Amelia?"

"I think it could hurt," I said quietly. "I think she knew that being angry would have eaten her up inside. So she tried to make the best of things. Even bad things."

He smiled and nodded. "Exactly!"

Slick threw her script on the floor and crossed her legs and her arms. She looked like a locked box.

It would take a crowbar to get her open.

I found Kate in the backyard after school. She spent a lot of time out there in the tree platform or messing around with the big wooden tiki we had brought from our old apartment complex.

"Hey, what's up?" I asked.

"I'm wishing on the tiki that I'll win the Miss Young Sunny California Pageant."

"Kate, how come you want this beauty pageant stuff so much?" I climbed up into the tree and looked down at her as she polished the tiki's tummy.

"I just do."

"I get that. But *why* do you?"

She looked up. "Because you don't want it. You get

all the attention with your ugly duckling stuff and I might as well be the invisible girl.''

I realized, with a flash, what had happened. I climbed down and sat next to her. "Can I make a wish now?" I asked.

"Okay." She didn't look at me.

I put my hand on the tiki's tummy and repeated the chant Kate had made up:

> *"Tiki, tiki standing tall,*
> *Grant my wishes,*
> *Grant them all."*

I closed my eyes and wished.

"What, what did you wish?" She grabbed my hand and squeezed.

"I'll never tell," I said with a smile. "You'll just have to wait and see!"

"You wished for me to get my wish, didn't you?"

She grabbed my neck and squeezed me so hard I thought I'd choke.

I unwound her. "I'm not telling!" I repeated. "And stop choking me, or I won't be able to take you to the preliminary pageant next week!"

She smiled. "I love you, Melia."

I recalled something we used to say when Kate was just learning to talk.

"We love *chuthers*!" I said.

"I remember that! It was for, 'we love each other,' right?"

"Right."

And that's what I had really wished for.

Forever.

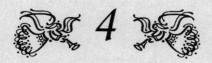

"**P**ass the potatoes, please."

"Here they come." I set the heavy bowl near Dad's plate. "Spoon on the right."

"Thanks." He plopped some on his plate at the two o'clock position. "I hear from your mom that Candy Crowley called you today."

"Yep. She wanted to tell me that the magazine that is going to print *Swan Songs* won't be having its first issue until summer. But they are definitely going to print it."

"What is this new magazine called again?" asked Mom.

"It's called *Inside Out*. They want it to compete with all the makeup and fashion magazines," I said. "You know, be about how girls are on the inside."

"That's a perfect title, then," said Dad. "Is she still planning to have you on her talk show again?"

"Uh-huh. She said we'll do it to coincide with the magazine debut, sometime next summer. All the people I interviewed are invited."

"Maybe she can have the winner of the Miss Sunny pageant on," said Kate with a wave of her fork. "That would be a good show, too."

"Especially if *you* win!" I teased.

"If I win, I'll be dumbstounded," she replied, her face serious.

Mom laughed. "Dumbfounded, honey."

"Well, I'll be dumbstounded if I get the role of Anne Frank," I said.

"You thought the reading went well, didn't you?" asked Dad.

"Pretty okay, I guess. There's still one more reading. I probably won't get the part."

He smiled and felt his Braille watch. "Frances, dear, we should get going."

"Oh, that's right, I nearly forgot." Mom wiped her mouth and pushed back from the table. "This pot roast isn't sitting too well with my stomach, anyway." She burped a little bit and excused herself. "Now, you girls clear up and do your homework. Daddy and I have a parents' meeting to attend at Bret Harte."

"Okay. Drive safely," I said.

"I will," said Dad.

I laughed.

"Hey, you can't drive, you're blind!" exclaimed Kate.

"I am? I forgot!" He picked her up and swung her around. She giggled and clung to him.

Sometimes I wished I was still a little girl.

After they left, Kate and I did the dishes. Except now we had a dishwasher! I could stop worrying about my hands turning into ugly old lobster claws from being dunked in hot, soapy water!

"I'll rinse, you load, okay?" I turned on the tap.

"Okay. I like loading. It's better than drying."

"Yeah. Isn't it nice living in a house?"

"Uh-huh. Only, I miss my imaginary friend. He stayed behind at our old apartment."

My surprise shot up into my eyebrows. I knew she meant Cyril, her guardian angel. "He stayed behind?"

"Yeah. I don't see him anymore. I left him behind for the next little girl."

"That was nice of you," I said. I turned to hand her a pan and, for a moment, I glimpsed Cyril.

He stood behind her, turning his hat in his hands. He leaned forward and whispered in her ear. She didn't respond.

I knew then that guardian angels miss us when we can't hear them anymore.

"*Won't* hear," corrected Lily in a whisper. "There is a big difference."

I thought about that as I finished the dishes.

* * *

I nervously fingered my script. This was the day of our final tryout.

There was Slick, pacing in the wings to my right. The tee shirt du jour said BACK OFF. Lily prodded me to do what I did next. I should have listened to the shirt instead.

"Slick?" I approached and stood aside, so she wouldn't pace right over me.

"What!" It did not sound as if she really wanted to know.

"I, ah, thought I would wish you good luck." The script slipped from my sweaty hands and I bent to retrieve it.

"Yeah. Right."

I shrugged and went back to my seat. A lot of good that did, I thought.

"More than you know, or she will show," reminded Lily, who promptly floated up behind the lights where I couldn't see her.

"Listen up people, everyone on stage for the final readings." Mr. Jacobs placed a single chair in the middle of the stage. "Sit here when I call your name. Please tell me the act and scene you have chosen before you begin." He consulted his clipboard. "Okay, Brian Siegel, you're up first. Brian is reading for the part of Anne's father, Otto Frank. All quiet, please!"

Brian read well. He even used an accent. I sucked in my breath and wished I did accents, too.

Each kid read, and the minutes ticked by. There was no joking around, probably because we were reading from the lives of people who were living through something that was not a joke.

I had the feeling we were honoring their memories, and to be honest, I had the feeling they were with us as we did.

My turn.

I sat in the chair and tried to be Anne Frank. I wanted to feel what she felt, so I tried to speak from her heart, not mine.

"Act two, scene four," I said. "It's the final scene when Anne is talking to Peter and they are looking out the skylight, just before the Nazis find them." I bowed my head, cleared my throat, and spoke:

" 'What a lovely, lovely day! Aren't the clouds beautiful? You know what I do when it seems as if I couldn't stand being cooped up for one more minute? I think myself out. I think myself on a walk in the park where I used to go with Pim. Where the jonquils and the crocuses and violets grow down the slopes. You know the most wonderful part about thinking yourself out? You can have it any way you like. You can have roses and violets and chrysanthemums all blooming at the same time . . . it's funny . . . I used to take it all for granted . . .' "

I closed the script and sat in the audience so I could watch the others. Most everyone did a good job, and I wondered how Mr. Jacobs would choose.

Slick was last. She clomped over to the chair. "This

is from act one, scene four. She's talking to her father about herself.'' Slick pushed her reddened hair out of her face and said:

'' 'I have a nicer side, Father . . . a sweeter, nicer side. But I'm scared to show it. I'm afraid that people are going to laugh at me if I'm serious. So the mean Anne comes to the outside and the good Anne stays on the inside, and I keep on trying to switch them around and have the good Anne on the outside and the bad Anne inside and be what I'd like to be . . . and might be . . . if only . . . only . . .' ''

Slick leaned back and popped a stick of gum in her mouth.

Mr. Jacobs scribbled something on his pad and my heart skipped a beat. Slick had done a good job, even I could see that. Maybe he was writing her name down for the part of Anne.

"Okay, troops," he said. "You all did a great job here, and I want you to know that I'm proud of you. I'll post the results tomorrow, and remember, every one of you will be involved in this play. The people on the stage can't do it without the people behind the scenes. We are all important here.''

Everyone mumbled their semi-agreement.

Mr. Jacobs' words stayed with me as I hurried to my locker. I knew he was right about things behind the scenes; they were invisible to the eye, but important.

I caught the bus outside the school, and headed for Greenblatt's Deli on Sunset Boulevard where I was meeting Richard for a snack. He was anxious to hear all about the play.

"Okay, spill, spill, how'd it go?" He leaned across the Formica table.

"I guess, maybe, it was okay . . ."

"That's the old positive spirit, Amelia!"

I laughed. "Well, you know how it is, I hate to get my hopes up."

"If you don't, who will?" He smiled at me and leaned back as Sol, our favorite waiter, shuffled over. "Hey, Sol, how's it going?"

"It's going, it's going, all the time. What can I do? I'm an old man." His gnarled hands curled around his pencil stub. "Eat. What are you wanting?"

"Pastrami on rye and a coke," Richard said.

"I'll have iced tea, Sol," I said, "and a toasted bagel."

"Cream cheese I will add, no charge." He scribbled laboriously. "Amelia, how is Katie, that little dumplink girl?"

"She's great. She's going to be in a beauty pageant pretty soon."

"Ach! Well, she should win with her hands down! Tell her I hope she wins."

"I will. Thanks."

Another customer waved at him and called for service.

"Your horses you should be holding! Can't you see I'm busy? I get to you, you wait. I'm an old man." He glared at the cringing lady and chugged off to the kitchen.

"He cracks me up," said Richard. "I'm amazed he has any customers."

"The food is great, that's why people come. And I think they kind of like him. He's not like anybody else, that's for sure."

"Kind of like me," said Richard.

"Exactly."

"So?"

"So, what?"

"The play! The play!" He stuck a toothpick in his mouth and promptly got it stuck in his braces.

I giggled and watched him try to get the splinters out. "It went fine. I know I did a good job. At least, I think I did. But Slick did a good job, too. And she's older than me, so I think she might get it."

"What'd her shirt say today?" he asked as he fished the last piece of wood from his mouth and wiped it on his shirt.

"Back Off."

"That's charming. And a good way to make friends, too. What is with her, anyway?"

Sol delivered our food and drinks and I sipped my tea. "I wish I knew. I really wish I knew."

"That can be arranged," whispered Lily into my left ear.

I sighed and blew bubbles into my glass. I would have

37

to remember to be more careful what I wished for!

"Anyway, that's what's going on. I mean, other than the regular school stuff. You know, juggling classes, combinations, and catastrophes." I smiled and thought of Shura. "I guess junior high is a BFD that you just get used to." I sighed, and put Shura back in my memory drawer. "So, how is it at your private school?"

"Snooty and expensive. In fact, that's the school motto." He grinned and tore into his sandwich.

"Any chance on your coming back to regular school?" I didn't want to come right out and say I missed him.

"So, you do miss me!"

I rolled my eyes. "I didn't say *that*."

"I read between the lines. It's another one of my gifts."

"Speaking of lines, as I was reading mine today, I was thinking that it would be nice if we all had a script for our lives. It would sure simplify things."

He smiled and wiped his mouth on a napkin. "May I quote?"

"Sure. I'm experiencing Shakespeare withdrawal symptoms." I shook my hands. "See?"

He sat up and cleared his throat. " 'All the world's a stage, and all the men and women merely players; they have their exits and their entrances, and one man in his time plays many parts . . .' "

Please, I asked silently, let me play my part well. Whatever it is.

38

* * *

That night the phone rang and I actually beat Kate to it. "Hello?"

"May I speak to Amelia Fleeman, please?"

"This is me."

"Hi, Amelia. It's Mr. Jacobs."

My breath got caught somewhere in my inside plumbing.

"You there?"

"I'm here, Mr. Jacobs."

"I'm calling only two people tonight, Amelia, and it's because I have a special request."

"I'll do it!" I said.

He laughed. "Wait a minute, wait a minute. You may regret that acceptance."

"Okay. What?"

"You and Grace were the only ones up for the part of Anne, as you know . . ."

"Yes?"

"And somehow, you each capture a different facet of her personality, so I want to try something new . . ."

"I don't get this at all! Which of us did you pick!" I wound the cord anxiously around my fingers.

"Both of you! We have four performances, two matinees and two evenings. You'll both do one of each."

"You mean we *both* got the part?"

"Indeed I do mean that. Is it okay with you?"

I told him it was. He thanked me and hung up to call Slick.

39

Lily smiled and took the phone from my hand. She set it gently in its cradle. "Isn't this handy, Amelia dear? You'll really get to know Slick now, won't you?"

"Yes," I mused, "it's almost as if someone wrote this into my script, isn't it?"

"I type fast," she said with a wicked smile.

Well, wicked with a dash of angel dust.

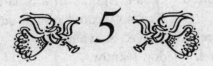

The next day, after school, I found Slick waiting at my locker.

"So," she crossed her thin arms and leaned against the wall of graffiti-covered lockers, "I guess you heard the news."

"Yes, I did." I busied myself in the depths of my locker, trying to gauge her reaction from her tone of voice, just as Dad had taught me.

"Brilliant stroke, if you ask me."

I peeked around my locker door. I was greeted with her tee shirt message: I'M NOT ANTI-SOCIAL. I JUST HATE YOU.

That pretty much set the tone.

"Maybe it will be fun," I suggested.

41

"Sure. It will be like we're stupid twins or something." She sighed and straightened up. "Jacobs says we should work together. You wanna?"

"Yeah! I think it's a good idea. That way we can understand the part better, since he thinks we kind of show both sides of Anne."

Slick snorted. "Yeah, right. I'm the dark side."

I smiled. "Oh, I'm not scared of the dark."

"Man, are you naive, or what?"

I shrugged. "I don't know."

"Well, you'll find out."

She fell into step beside me and we walked together down the hall. Her combat boots made a loud *stomp* in the corridor. My sneakers whispered along beside it.

"Do you take a bus home?" I asked.

"Nah. Matt, my boyfriend, he picks me up." She sounded proud. "He won't even let me so much as talk to another guy."

"You have a boyfriend old enough to DRIVE?"

She laughed and lit a cigarette as soon as we hit the sidewalk outside the school. "What of it?"

"Nothing of it, really. How old are you?"

"Fourteen."

"How old's he?"

"Seventeen."

"Wow."

"I like older guys. Guys my own age are jerks, freaks, and babies." She waved at a low, black car that pulled up. The windows were shaking from the loud music inside. "Here he is. You wanna ride or somethin'?"

She might as well have offered me a ride to a grunge concert. No way I was getting in that car.

"No, no, thanks. I have to take the bus some-where . . . somewhere special today." I scribbled my phone number on a torn piece of notebook paper. "Maybe you could call tonight, though. We could work on the play after school, or over the weekend."

"Yeah. Just so long as it's not on Friday night. I hang out then."

"Okay." I usually baby-sit then, I thought.

She climbed down into the noisy, black hole and sped away.

I got on my bus and transferred to the number 10. That was the bus that would take me to Beth Olam Cemetery, and to my best friend, Shura Najinsky.

The cemetery grounds were quiet. Of course.

Shura's grave had been well tended since I last vis-ited, right after her funeral. I could see her grandmoth-er's loving touch in the flowers and neatly trimmed grass.

"Hi, Shur." I settled myself on the grass and stared at her gravestone. I knew Shura wasn't in the ground or anything like that, but I figured she might be hang-ing around. You know, to see the people who came to visit her.

43

"I miss you. It's a BFD that you're gone." I paused and sighed. "Nobody can ever take your place. That is for sure."

I told Shura all about Lily and Slick and what was happening in my family. And I felt better. Sometimes you don't need an answer. You just need to talk. I think the words need to be set free, and then you're lighter.

Lily appeared just as I was getting up to leave.

"I thought you'd like to be alone for a bit," she said softly.

"Yes, I did need it. Thanks."

"You are welcome." She extended her closed hand. "I bring you good tidings from Shura."

"What?"

"Take this. It is from Shura. She wishes you to have it." She wiggled her hand. "Come, come."

I put out my palm and Lily dangled something in the air, and let it drop. I gazed at it. Tears sprang to my eyes.

"It's my talisman," I whispered. "The one I got from the kids at the blind school." I looked up at Lily, confused. "But I buried this here for Shura to have. Didn't she want it?"

"She loved it, Amelia, as she loves you, but she wants you to have it back. It is a special object to you and to her, but as the human, you are the rightful guardian of such things."

44

I smiled and put it around my neck. "I guess Shura couldn't exactly wear it, huh?"

"Shura's spirit is a large one. She wears that. It is all she needs."

"Can you talk to her? See her?" I couldn't hide the jealousy in my voice.

"Not as we do here on the earth. I feel her wishes and I sense her spirit. It is a seeing beyond sight."

"I see, I think."

"Your talisman is lovely. Read it to me, won't you?" Lily plucked a stray leaf from my hair.

"It says, 'Wait for the day that maketh all things clear.' It comes from the quote over the main entrance at Bret Harte school for the blind."

"Oh, yes. 'Night is too young, O friend. Day is too near; Wait for the day that maketh all things clear. Not yet, O friend, not yet.' "

"How'd you know that?"

Her laughter rained lightly around us. "Oh, Amelia, need you ask?"

I laughed. "No, I need not."

"Good. We are making progress!"

Maybe Lily and I were progressing, but Slick and I were not.

She didn't show up for two after school appointments we had to work on the play. I finally got her on the phone Friday afternoon.

"Hi, Slick. It's me, Amelia . . ."

45

Silence.

"You know," I continued, "from school? From the play?"

"I know. I know. What?"

"I've almost got the part memorized, but it would help if we could work on it, don't you think?"

"I guess. Especially since I haven't even opened the stupid thing."

"You haven't?"

"No. I haven't. Chill. I'll do it."

"Well, can you do it tonight, or are you going out? I mean, I know it's Friday and everything."

"Nah. Matt has to work. So I can do it, at least for a while, till he gets off."

"Do you want to come here, to my house?"

"No way. You come here."

"What's the address?"

She rattled it off and I wrote it down. "Okay. I'll see you tonight after dinner. When do you eat?"

"Whenever I feel like it."

"Oh. Well, we always eat at six, so I'll come around seven. Okay?"

She had already hung up.

Mom dropped me off at five to seven. "You be careful, honey. It's a little bit rough over here, just off the Sunset Strip. You call me from inside her house, and don't wait outside if it's dark. Daddy and I will come back to get you."

46

"Oh, Mom, for heaven's sake. I'll be fine. We'll be inside."

"Good." She waved and drove away.

I found the right apartment and knocked. Someone let me in. And it wasn't Slick.

"Hi. Um, is Slick Jamison here?"

"She's in the back. She'll be right out." A short, blonde girl, heavily made up and dressed a lot like Slick, stood aside so I could go in. "You're from the play, right?" She flopped onto an old couch, picked up the TV remote, and surfed between music channels.

"Yes. Do you go to our school?"

"Yeah." She looked up at me. "Sit down or something. You make me nervous, hovering over there."

I sat. "I haven't seen you around school."

"You wouldn't have. I got suspended for fighting." She grinned. "But it was worth it. I won."

On that note, I got up and wandered around. I stopped in the hallway at an old bookshelf that was littered with photographs: all of them were of Slick when she was younger. There she was, smiling (a new sight to me) and posing with her soccer team. There was another of her doing ballet as a little girl. And a bunch of her out on a lake, fishing with an older man. There were a couple of trophies for a girls' softball team, too.

"Those were my geek years."

I jumped. "Oh, hi, Slick, I was just noticing. You don't look like a geek to me."

47

"Yeah? Well, I was."

"Is that your father?"

"Nope. My grandpa. He died. I live with my grandma. She's at work." She fingered one of the fishing photos. "Gramps was a good old guy."

I wanted to ask about her parents, but knew I shouldn't. I had a father who had left, and I didn't like to be asked about it. Maybe it was the same for Slick.

"Didja meet my friend Spooky?"

"Her name is Spooky?"

"Not her real name. Her street name."

"Oh."

We stood awkwardly for a moment.

"Listen, I really gotta dye my hair tonight." She ran her hands through her dirty hair. "The roots are showing. It doesn't take long. Can you, like, hang with us while we go get the dye at the drugstore? Then we could work on the play while the stuff sets into my hair."

"I guess." I knew my mom would not want me to go out, but what could I do?

"Great. Hey, Spook, let's go get the stuff." Slick jabbed her thumb at me. "She's coming too."

"Whatever." Spooky got up and grabbed her purse.

Slick pulled a sweater over her WELCOME TO MY NIGHTMARE tee shirt.

We set off into the night, and suddenly I wasn't so comfortable in the dark. I trailed behind them and felt about as useful as a third shoe.

48

That is, until we got to the drugstore. Then I was very necessary.

We walked up and down the aisles until we came to the long row of hair care products. Pictures of pretty women smiled up at us from the boxes, their hair shining like no hair I had ever seen.

"Here," whispered Slick. "You look real innocent. Just slide this box into your shirt." She shoved a box of Caribbean Red hair dye at me.

I shook my head. "*No*! No way!"

"Shhhhhh," warned Spooky. "The guy will hear you!"

"No," I whispered. "I'm not going to steal. And you guys better not, either."

"I'm broke, how else am I supposed to get it?" asked Slick.

I stared at her. "Then you don't get it until you can pay."

"I don't like to wait. I'm not good at it."

I watched, in shock, as she stepped behind Spooky and slid the box under her shirt and into the band of her pants.

"Okay, now be cool. We'll buy some gum to throw him off, and we're out of here."

We almost made it.

"Young ladies!" boomed a voice.

We turned to face a security guard.

"Hey, man! We gotta go!" said Spooky.

He grabbed all of us at once. "Oh, you gotta go, all

49

right. You gotta go to the police station until we notify your parents that you were shoplifting.'' He pointed at a camera hidden behind a Coke sign. ''I've got you girls on 'Candid Camera.' ''

''Wait, sir, I didn't do anything!'' I started to cry.

''Sorry, kid.'' He dragged us to a room in the back. ''You're here. You are involved.''

It was a long ride to the police station.

6

The police station was big and gray and cold.

Kind of how I felt inside.

"Name!" barked the police officer behind the front desk.

We gave our names, addresses, and phone numbers.

It felt as if we were Dorothy, the Tin Woodsman, and the Scarecrow when they first faced the Wizard of Oz.

"Since you girls are juveniles, we won't put you in the holding cell. At least, not this time." He eyed us disapprovingly. "Although, it might be a good lesson for all of you to spend a night with the hookers and the drunks. Maybe scare some sense into you."

Slick stared at him with narrowed eyes. "You don't scare me."

"You scare me," I squeaked. The Cowardly Lion in me was coming out!

He shook his head and shuffled the many papers on his desk. "Sally!" he called to a woman across the room. "Put these ladies in the interrogation room to wait for their proud parents to come and get 'em. Don't let them so much as go to the bathroom alone."

"Sure, boss," said Sally. "Come along, girls. Let's not annoy the sergeant anymore."

"Ma'am?" I said as we walked down the hall.

"Yes?"

"Can I wait in a different room from them?" I shied away from Slick and Spooky and hugged the far wall.

"Trouble in the ranks, huh?" she asked.

"You could say that," I said.

"Well, if there's a room free, then I'm sure it's okay. Lemme check." She opened a door and stuck her head in. "Okey-dokey, kid, you sit in here. Give you time to think things over and decide what to tell your folks. Take my advice; the truth will set you free."

I smiled my gratitude and swallowed my anxiety. It didn't taste very good.

"Hey," called Slick as the door closed, "I didn't plan this, you know."

I turned my back on her and sat down in the cold, hard chair. "I hate you, Slick Jamison!" I said, slapping my hand on the table in front of me.

"Hatred only poisons the vessel that holds it," said Lily, who sat across from me and patted my hand.

52

"I don't care! Look what she did to me! I am in a police station, a convict practically, and it is all her fault, and I hate her! And her red hair! And that nose ring!"

"Amelia, Amelia," Lily soothed. "What was it you said about Anne Frank and her attitude toward the Nazis?"

"This is different."

"No, it's not." She steepled her fingers and looked into my eyes. "Is it?"

I squirmed under her gaze. "Well, it feels different now," I grumbled.

"Exactly, my dear. You don't learn it until you live it. Perhaps we should be grateful for these lessons that we dislike."

"Grateful?" I stared at her. "Not only am I not grateful, I don't want to be friends with Slick. Not ever. Never."

"All right."

A smile rose from my depths. "You mean, I don't have to help her anymore? I'm done? Off the angelic hook?"

"If you think that walking away from something difficult means 'off the hook,' then indeed you are." Lily smiled. She didn't seem angry or anything.

I started to breathe a sigh of relief. But it got caught. Somewhere halfway between my heart and my head.

"But what will happen to Slick?" I asked.

"Oh, that will be no concern of yours," she said reassuringly. "You'll be fine, your life will go well."

Something didn't feel right. I started to speak, but Lily put her finger to her lips. "Shhh. There is someone here for you."

I steeled myself to face my parents as the door slowly opened.

"Hello?" An older lady, wearing a waitress uniform, and worn-down orthopedic shoes, came in and closed the door behind her. "Have you seen my granddaughter?"

"Mrs. Jamison?" I asked.

"Yes." She looked confused. "They told me this room is where Grace could be found. Is that right?"

Lily raised her eyebrows at me. The word "grace" was more than just a name to her. And, I realized, to me as well.

"Grace will come soon," I said. "Why don't you sit down? You look tired." I pulled a chair out for her.

"Thank you kindly, my dear." She pulled a hankie out of the cuff of her uniform and wiped her eyes. "I am just sick with worry over that child. And, now, here she is at the police station." She shook her head slowly. "I just don't know if I can handle her anymore."

"Could she go live with her mom or dad? Maybe they could help," I suggested.

"Her mother died. Her father, my son, John Jamison, is remarried and living in Eugene, Oregon. Grace don't want no part of him or his new family. He wants her to live there and even had her stay last summer with him, but she threatened to run away. She says he's too strict." She sighed. "We don't know what to do about her. It

54

was not bad when my Sam was alive, but now I'm widowed, and I can't hardly handle her.''

"Has she always been in trouble?''

"Oh, no, not at all! Why she used to be active and happy and involved in all sorts of sports. She loved fishin' and playin' ball.'' She smiled at her memories of a younger, graceful granddaughter. "She started acting up when she was twelve or so.'' She wiped her eyes. "All of a sudden she didn't like how she looked, and she complained that the boys and girls at school picked on her. But I don't know why. I truly don't.''

"Oh. I think I know what that's like.''

Mrs. Jamison looked at me, her eyes full of hope. "Are you a friend of my granddaughter?''

The room was quiet as I gathered my thoughts.

"Yes, Ma'am, I am. At least, I'm trying to be.''

"You seem like a nice girl. Maybe you could help her. She seems so unhappy, and I don't know why. Not for the life of me. I just know that unhappy children do unhappy things.''

"I could try to help. But I don't know if she'll let me,'' I said. A tingle went up my spine and I felt Lily kiss my cheek.

"Oh, please don't be put off by her hard look. That's not really my baby.'' The old lady rummaged around in her purse and pulled out her wallet. She flipped to the picture section. "Come and look here. This is my little Gracie when she was nine.''

I looked down at the photo and caught my sudden tears before they fell.

It was a picture of Slick all dressed up for Halloween. She was an angel. Wings, halo, and all.

"That's who she really is," whispered the grandmother, taking my no longer unwilling hand in hers. "There's an angel underneath."

"There always is, I guess." I patted her shoulder. "Thank you for reminding me."

Just then, Sally came back in.

"Oh, here you are, Mrs. Jamison. Now, how'd you ever end up in here?"

Lily smiled and held the door open for them.

As they went out, Mom and Dad came in, the cool night air still clinging to their coats.

"Oh, thank goodness you're okay!" Mom grabbed me and pressed her cheek against mine.

I squeezed her back and looked at Dad over her shoulder. He felt my gaze and extended his arms. I fell into them.

He held me and whispered, "Sometimes you need a Dad hug. To be used in case of emergency."

I nodded and let myself be held.

"I know this seems bad, but it isn't like it looks . . ." I stepped back and tried to explain my predicament.

"We know," said Mom. "They showed us the tape from the drugstore surveillance camera. It was clear that you weren't involved."

"Will this go on my record?" I asked.

"No," said Dad. "The police don't want to charge you. They just want you to be aware that when you're with kids who get into trouble, it will affect you as well."

"I'll be more careful," I said. "Believe me!"

"We do believe you. And we believe in you," said Mom.

As we left, I saw Spooky's parents. Her mother was beautiful, in a red velvet dress and ropes of pearls. Her father was wearing a tux. They were yelling at Spooky.

"We were pulled out of an important business event for this!" fumed her father. "I have had it with this nonsense from you!"

Spooky looked at him, her face a blank.

"Why don't you just stay at home with all the nice things we have for you?" pleaded her mother. "You could watch cable, or play videos, or swim in the pool, or go in the exercise room . . ."

"Yeah," said Spooky. "Me and the maid. That should be fun."

"Your gratitude is underwhelming," said her father with a sad shake of his head.

I watched as they filed out the door and disappeared into the darkness.

"I have an idea," Dad said suddenly. "Fran, will you two wait for just a few minutes? I want to speak to the sergeant."

"Of course, Noel, but what . . . ?"

"I'll explain it later—*if* it works out." He made his way carefully down the unfamiliar hall.

"Mom, I have one more thing to do, too. Okay?"

"That depends." She slipped an arm around my waist. "Is it legal?"

"Mom!"

"Well, you never know. I don't want you to end up like the gals in those old prison movies."

I laughed. "Yeah, that's me, the hardened criminal from *Women Behind Bars*."

"Okay, go ahead, but hurry. Daddy won't be long and we have to pick Kate up from Aunt Jean and Uncle Leo's house."

"Oh! I nearly forgot about her! Where did you tell her I was?"

"In jail," said Mom.

"You didn't!"

"Of course not, Amelia. Now, scoot!"

I scooted down the hall to the room where Slick had been deposited. She was still there. All alone.

"Hi. Where's your grandmother?" I closed the door and sat across from her.

"She's signing some papers. I think they want to send me to juvenile detention or something."

"I don't think so," I said. "I think we get to leave."

"I wouldn't mind staying." Slick sighed and leaned back in her chair.

"In here?"

"Yeah. In here." She crossed her arms on the table and buried her head.

"Why?"

"Because it's safe in here. There's dragons out there," came the muffled reply.

"I don't get it."

"Why am I not surprised?" She sat up and stared at me. She pulled out a stick of gum and folded it slowly into her mouth before she continued, "See, back in the Middle Ages there were these old guys who drew maps of the world as far as they knew it to go, and around the edges of what they knew they wrote in big 'ol black letters: HERE THERE BE DRAGONS."

"But there aren't really any . . ."

"Just cuz *you* don't see them in your world, doesn't mean they don't exist in mine," she said.

She had me there.

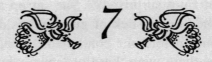

7

"It was really nice of your parents to give us their season tickets, Richard." I walked carefully in my two-inch high heels toward the entrance of the Dorothy Chandler Pavilion.

"No sweat. They had a big faculty meeting, and they didn't want the tickets to go to waste. I wasn't sure that you'd like classical music, though." He pulled at his tie and grabbed my arm as we headed up the steps. "Watch out, it's kind of slippery here."

"Thanks, you are such a gentleman."

"Yeah. We're a dying breed, according to my dad. So, you do like classical music then?"

"I didn't listen to it much until my mom got married

to Mr. C. He listens to it a lot. He says that music is what people use when they can't find any more words.''

''As the Bard said, 'If music be the food of love, play on!' ''

I turned and looked at him. He was blushing, but I wasn't sure why.

We walked through the huge glass doors and I gasped as they closed silently behind us. ''Wow. Look at this place!''

''I used to call it the Dorothy *Chandelier* Pavilion,'' he said, gesturing at the decor.

''No wonder. Look at all those lights! And those mirrors reflect everything and make it look even more spectacular.'' I straightened my sleeves. ''And look at how everyone is dressed,'' I whispered. ''They look almost as good as the building.''

''Yeah, only smaller.'' He took my hand with a smile and led me to the seats.

I sunk into the velvety cushion of seat 3-C and sighed. ''So, this is how the other half lives!''

''That's right. You ex-cons don't know what you're missing. The straight and narrow isn't so bad.'' He smiled and gave me a sideways glance.

''Geez, just advertise it, why don't you?''

''Nah. You are my date, after all.'' He glanced quickly at me. ''If that's okay with you.''

''Sure!'' I busied myself with my program, but smiled at my promotion from pal to date.

"So, finish telling me what happened. My mom came in just when we were getting to the part where your dad went to talk to the police sergeant."

"Oh, yeah." I smoothed my dress and thought for a second. "Dad asked the police if he could get Slick and Spooky involved in the buddy program over at Bret Harte. He wants them to come over after school and on Saturday mornings. You know, sort of like community service instead of them getting some other kind of punishment."

"What did the police say?"

"They thought it was a good idea. The sergeant told Dad that he thinks a lot of kids who get in trouble really just need something to keep them busy."

"It's gotta be better than hanging around on Sunset Boulevard."

"That's what I think, too." Somehow I knew that just about anything was better than that!

The orchestra started to make scratchy noises and the talking in the auditorium faded away.

"Is that the first song?" I whispered.

"No. They're just warming up. The best is yet to come!"

I smiled. I was just warming up, too. So maybe the best was yet to come with Slick.

A tingle went up my spine and I glanced up into the cavernous hall. Sure enough, there was Lily dancing on air to the music rising below her.

When I got home, Katie was hanging around in my room. Actually, she was right in my bed.

"Did you have fun?" She sat up and watched as I undressed.

"I really did! I wasn't sure if I'd like it, but I did. They did music called 'The Four Seasons,' and you could really tell which season was which just by the sound. It was beautiful!" I threw my dress on a chair, thought better of it, and hung it up.

"Amelia, when is it time for my beauty pageant? You didn't forget, did you?"

Actually, I had hoped she would forget. I pulled on my nightgown and climbed into bed. "I didn't forget. The preliminary pageant is this weekend, and if you make it there, you get to go on to the Miss Sunny pageant on Valentine's Day."

"Good. I can't wait!" She snuggled down under the covers. "Can I sleep in here tonight?"

"Okay. Did you go to the bathroom?"

"Uh-huh."

"I'll turn out the light then." We didn't say anything for a few minutes. Then I said, "Listen, Katie, you know, even if you get through the preliminary pageant, you might not win Miss Sunny."

"I know."

"Just so you know."

"I know I might not win. That's okay."

I patted her hand. "Good."

"But, I *might* win." She giggled and hugged herself. "And that would be okay, too!"

I laughed and tickled her. "Okay, okay, Queen Kate, go to sleep, we have school tomorrow."

She squeezed her eyes shut. "I'm going to dream of being Miss Sunny. You stay awake and watch me, maybe my dream will appear over my head in a big bubble!"

"No way! It's not like a TV show! Dreams are . . ." I furrowed my brow. "Well, they're like pretend."

"But I can see them. So I don't see why you can't see them, too. Maybe you just need to look with dreamy eyes."

I laughed. "Okay, I'll try."

"Goody." She turned over. "Okay, here I go!"

"Okay! Don't dream of dragons!"

"I won't. I don't like dragons!"

I stayed awake for a while, but I didn't see my sister's dreams.

I did think of dragons, though. And I wondered what Slick was dreaming of.

My question was answered at school the next day.

"I had a lousy weekend!" said Slick as she clomped into play rehearsal and threw her stuff on a chair.

"Why?" I put down my script and looked up. We were early and had the stage to ourselves.

"Well, let's see now, first I get hauled off to the police, then I get told by Gram that I can't go out at night,

64

then I get the good news that I have to nursemaid a bunch of blind kids. And I find out that only I have to, because Spooky got out of it somehow.''

"The kids at Bret Harte are nice kids!'' I said defensively.

"I don't care. I hate all this stuff. All these stupid rules.'' She looked around and furtively lit a cigarette.

"Hey, you can't smoke in here, it's against the rules.''

"What is it with you and rules?'' She blew smoke into the stale air. "Don't you get sick of that crap?''

I had to think for a second. I had always followed most of Mom's rules, and the school rules, but I wasn't sure why. "Well, I guess it's because rules make me feel like I'm something, or someone, that is worth protecting.''

She looked at me thoughtfully. "I never thought of it like that.''

I leaned forward eagerly. "Really?''

"And I wouldn't, either, because that's the biggest crock I have ever heard in my life. Rules are to control. That's it.''

"Fine.'' I put my nose back into my script.

"I used to follow the rules too.''

"Oh, yeah? When was that?'' I didn't look up because I had the feeling she didn't want to be confronted with my eyes.

"All the time when I was a little kid. But it got me nowhere. I was a goody-goody with no friends and no social life who was afraid to leave the nice, safe shallow water . . . then I decided to take a chance! Jump right into the deep water and stop following the rules. I figured maybe that would be more interesting.''

"Is it?''

"Yeah.'' She snorted and blew smoke out her nostrils. "Look at me now. I have a boyfriend and I have people to hang with. And I have fun.''

"Guess that depends on your definition of fun,'' I said, recalling the police station.

She put out the cigarette and straightened her black tee shirt. "That's right. And my definition of fun is to hang with people who like me, and don't make fun of how I look, and who don't leave me. And I have all that now.''

"Sounds good.''

"Because it is good. You should try it.''

"No, I don't think so. Because you forgot one thing.''

"Like what?'' she asked as the other kids started to arrive. "Name it.''

"Dragons,'' I replied softly. "I hear there are dragons out there in the deep.''

Mr. Jacobs' arrival cut off her reply, but I noticed she was blushing.

"Okay, troops, let's have our second script reading today. I want to hear the fruits of your weekend labors!'' Mr. Jacobs positioned himself at the head of the long table and we each took a chair.

"Who should read Anne?'' asked Slick.

"This time, I want each of you to take an act. Grace, you go first."

I thought, after the weekend's excitement, that she would blow it. But she didn't.

Then I thought I would. But I didn't either.

We both seemed to understand the confused feelings of the young girl who hid in an attic when she was thirteen years old.

I guess there have always been dragons in the world that you sometimes have to hide from.

I thought Kate would bust a gut as we drove up the street toward the Miss Young Sunny California preliminary pageant.

"We're here! We're here! Stop, Mommy! I have to get out!" She bounced on the seat and pulled at her seat belt.

"Kate, sit still this instant, or I'll have to stop the car. That bouncing is distracting and it's making me nauseous."

"Me, too," I complained.

"Okay." Kate went as stiff as a statue.

"Well, you can breathe for heaven's sake," said Mom.

"Not if you want me to be still, too." She jutted her chin and crossed her arms.

"Good luck, Amelia," said Mom as she pulled into a parking space. "And thank you so much!"

"Sure, Mom. Maybe it'll even be fun."

"Dream on!" said Mom with a laugh.

"I will, Mommy," replied Kate. "I'll dream on to the crown!"

"Come on, Queenie, let's get in there. Musn't be late," I said as I took her hand and watched Mom drive away.

"That's right." She let go of my hand and pushed me, like a little tugboat, toward the doors.

If only determination counted, she would surely win.

I handed Kate's form to a well-dressed lady standing guard at the door. "Is there an entry check in here, hon? And have your parents signed the form?" she asked cheerfully.

"Yes, Ma'am."

"Good enough!" She put Kate's application in the "F" box, pinned a sunny name tag to her, and directed us to the next step: "Personal Appearance."

I stood aside as another lady (with lots of makeup) inspected my sister. "My, my, but you do have lovely skin, Kate. Maybe in the big pageant you could use a little makeup."

"Oh, my mom will veto *that*," I said.

"Really?" She batted false eyelashes my way. "What a shame. All the little misses do it, dear. It just brightens their looks under those harsh lights. You should take every advantage, you know."

"Amelia, I want to take every vantage!" said Kate.

"We'll see," I hedged.

Apparently Kate passed because we were sent to a room marked "Personality."

"You've got plenty of this," I reassured her. "It should be a snap."

She snapped her fingers.

I smiled some encouragement at her and waited outside, as no one was permitted in except the contestant.

Lily touched my elbow and I turned to her. "I don't feel good about all this," I worried.

"I know. But Katie does. That's what matters."

"If you say so." I paced up and down the hall. Lily paced, too, only she floated.

"Let's go over here," she said, floating ahead of me and around a corner.

"Okay." I followed and was stopped short by a grating voice.

"Tiffany, why didn't you smile the way I showed you!" A woman and a little girl were standing in front of me. The woman continued, "You can't show your gums and you can't smile too full, it will give you laugh lines."

"I did it right, Mommy," cried the child. "At least I think I did."

"Well, Missy, apparently you didn't. I saw the judges' paper. They marked you off for poor smile."

Tiffany hung her head. "So I can't be in the big pageant?"

"No. You can not. Maybe next time you will be more careful!"

"I think you have a pretty smile!" I said.

They both looked up, startled.

"Are you a judge?" asked the mother.

"No."

"Then who cares what you think?"

"I care," said Tiffany, handing me a small, grateful smile as her mother dragged her away.

Lily watched them go. "Sometimes," she said slowly, "it just breaks my heart to watch humans."

"Mine, too," I said.

"Amelia! Come quick!"

I nearly jumped out of my skin as I ran down the hall toward the sound of my little sister's frantic voice.

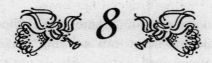

8

"**I** made it! I made it! They said I get to come to the Miss Sunny pageant on Valentine's Day! I could be the Queen!" Kate ran toward me, trailing exuberance like a jet stream.

"You did? That's great, you must be really excited now! You're one step closer to *Queendom*." I hugged her and looked at my watch. "Listen, we better get going, we have to take the bus home and if we hurry we can catch the next one."

"I can't wait to tell Mommy and Daddy!"

She didn't have to wait long. The Miss Sunny pageant was the main topic of conversation that night over dinner.

"I'm happy to hear that things went so well," said Dad.

"Yep!" declared Kate, waving a chicken leg, "I passed with flying colors!"

"Speaking of flying colors," I said, "they told me that Kate should wear some makeup when she goes to the big pageant."

"Oh, no! I draw the line there!" said Mom. "I won't have them pushing her into wearing makeup, or into wearing an inappropriate dress. She is too young."

"I'm not too young! A lot of the girls there were already wearing makeup and fancy dresses. I was the plainest person of all." Kate's eyes welled up with tears.

"But they still chose you," said Dad quietly. "I think maybe you can make them see beyond the flash and the glitter. Your personality is quite glittery just as it is!" He smiled and sipped his iced tea.

"I don't know about that," said Kate doubtfully. "Not everybody is as smart as you, Daddy."

"That is for sure," I said.

"I couldn't agree more," said Mom, patting his hand.

"Come on, now, you three, I'm going to get a swelled head."

"I hope I don't get one," said Kate.

"Don't worry," I said. "I'll see to it that you don't!"

"And I'll see to it you don't wear a mask of makeup," said Mom. "Why, I don't even let Amelia wear any, except on very special occasions!"

I looked at Kate's crestfallen face.

Dad cleared his throat. "Fran?"

"Yes?"

"Maybe to Katie, this is a very special occasion."

"We could make sure it's just a teeny bit of makeup," I suggested.

"The teeniest, tiniest bit," whispered Kate. "Almost invisible."

Mom sighed. "Okay. A little mascara, a little pale pink lipstick, and that is it. If you want your cheeks to be pink, just pinch them."

"Thanks, Mommy!" Kate ran around the table and hugged her.

"You're welcome. I think."

Kate made her way over to Dad. "I'm here by your side, get ready for a hug."

"I'm always ready for one of those," he said.

Kate crawled up onto his lap. "You know, Mommy, the lady at the pageant said I have to wear a special outfit that has a theme to it when I come back the next time. And this year the theme is, 'The Freedom of Flight.' "

"Clothes with a flying theme?" asked Dad. "You mean we have to dress you up like a bird?"

"How about a chicken?" I asked, as I finished off the last of mine.

"No way, Jose! Chickens are goofy looking," said Kate. "Besides, it doesn't have to be a bird. It can be anything that makes people feel free!" She got up and swooped around the room.

"I know how you should dress!" I said.

73

"How?" She stopped flying.

"Like an angel," I said. "They fly, and the costume would be appropriate for a little girl."

"Perfect!" said Mom. "That's a relief. It shouldn't entail much sewing."

"Well, Kate?" I asked. "Is an angel okay with you?"

"An angel is just the very right thing," she said. "I've always loved angels!"

Cyril appeared behind her and smiled.

"Speaking of angels," said Dad. "I was wondering if you would be an angel for me, Amelia?"

"Sure. What do you need?"

"Would you come over to Bret Harte tomorrow and show Slick the ropes? I'm sure all your years of volunteer experience will be helpful."

I looked at Lily, whose hand must be in this. She smiled and held her hands up, in mock innocence.

She was sure sneaky for an angel.

"Okay, Dad. It will have to be after play rehearsal, though."

"I know, Grace, I mean Slick, mentioned that when I spoke with her. Maybe you two could just come over together. It would give you a chance to get to know her better. I get the feeling she could use a friend."

"Okay." I got up and took my plate to the kitchen. I suddenly had the urge to scrub something. Hard.

"Don't worry," said Lily from over my shoulder. "I'll give her a little nudge. You could use the help."

"I know." I put down the scrubbie and stared out the window. "Being an angel is a messy business sometimes, isn't it?"

"Yes. I guess it's like a garden—if you want flowers, you have to get your hands dirty."

The next afternoon found Slick and me arguing outside the school after rehearsal.

"I don't think we should ride with your boyfriend," I said. "We can catch a bus that takes us right to the front steps of Bret Harte."

She crossed her arms. "Look, it's bad enough I have to go. What is the big deal if Matt takes us? You afraid of him, or what?"

"No. I just value my eardrums."

"Big whoop. I'll get him to turn the stereo down. *Okay*?" She kicked a rock with her combat boot. I had the distinct impression she would rather be kicking me.

"Oh, all right." I checked my watch. "He better be here in a few minutes though, or we'll be late."

"So?"

"So? That would be rude. The kids are waiting for us. Maybe my dad, too."

"Whatever." She pulled out a pack of gum and waved it at me. "Want some?"

"No, thanks."

We stood awkwardly for a few minutes.

"I think the play is coming along really well, don't you?" I asked.

"It's okay."

"Are you nervous about putting it on for everybody?"

"Kinda. Are you?"

"A little." I swallowed and continued, "Especially that part where Anne has to kiss Peter."

She stopped chewing and turned to me. "Oh, no, don't tell me?"

"What?"

"You have never been kissed, have you?" She whooped and danced around the sidewalk. "What a crack-up!"

I stood like stone, waiting for her to finish.

"Well? Am I right?"

"You're right."

"Hah! Don't you feel like a freak?" She grinned and poked me.

"No. Do you?" I blinked back my anger and embarrassment.

"Why should I feel weird? I've been kissed and then some." She stood taller.

"That's what I meant," I said quietly. "You act like you've won something. I think you've lost something."

She shook her head and bit her fingernails. "I don't know what you're talkin' about. Anyway, here comes Matt."

The stereo on wheels pulled up to the curb. Slick opened the door and asked him to turn down the volume. He growled, but he did it.

The car stopped shaking and I got into the back seat.

"No ride until you pay up," said Matt, pushing his long, dark hair out of his eyes.

I looked away as Slick kissed him. I had to look away for quite awhile.

They didn't talk much as we drove along. I wondered if it was just because I was there.

"Here it is," I said. "This is the school."

Matt pulled the car over with an exaggerated movement of wheels and rubber. "Okay. Heft it out, girls. And you better get to the 7-Eleven by eight, Slick," he instructed as we got out. "Cuz I'm not waitin' around. I don't want to miss that party."

"Sure, Matt," she said. "As long as my Grandma doesn't get home early."

He screeched away.

"I thought you were supposed to stay in at night," I said as we walked up the path toward the entrance.

"Listen!" she said. "You are not my keeper, okay? So just get the idea out of your head that you are. I don't need your help. Or your stupid suggestions."

"Okay, okay," I said. "I was just worried about your grandma, really. She seemed like a sweet old lady."

"She is." Slick seemed to calm down. "She just doesn't get why I have to do what I do. Life is not like it was when she was a girl. We have divorces, drugs, and destruction now. It's a lot more complicated."

"Yeah," I agreed. "Things are hard. For lots of people." I opened the doors to Bret Harte. "Let's go. The kids are waiting."

Slick paused and read the message over the door. "What's with that?"

"It's kind of their motto."

"I don't get it. They can't even read it."

"That's true. I wondered about that at first, too, but then I found out they have to memorize it."

She seemed to puzzle over it. " 'Wait for the day that maketh all things clear. Not yet, O friend, not yet.' " She shook her head. "I still don't get it. It will never be clear for them, if you ask me. I mean, they *are* blind." She stomped ahead of me.

I took her into the office and explained the Braille equipment. Next I showed her the room where they read books onto tape.

"See the markers on the walls?" I asked when we were back in the hallway.

She nodded.

"That's so the kids can feel their way along. Until they get a sense of things."

We went into the big playroom, where Dad had established an after-school program. The kids were laughing and talking and doing art projects.

"Hi, Mrs. Weiss," I said to the teacher on duty, who was also blind. "I'm here for the buddy program."

Mrs. Weiss turned to us. "Hello, Amelia. How nice to see you again. And who is your friend?"

Slick looked surprised that a blind person could "see" her.

"This is Grace Jamison. Do you have someone you want her assigned to?"

"Yes. Your father wanted Grace to be a buddy to Eloise Simpkins." She turned her body toward the room. "Eloise! Please come up front, dear. Your buddy is here."

"You're not gonna leave me alone with her, are you?" Slick grabbed my hand for a second.

"No." I laughed. "But, she won't bite."

"At least, not anymore," said Mrs. Weiss. "Some of the children haven't learned how to handle their anger at being blind. Those are the biters."

Slick swallowed her gum.

A small, thin, dark-haired girl slowly approached us, using a strip of plastic on the floor to guide her feet.

Her eyes were not covered with dark glasses, and they seemed to look everywhere and nowhere.

"Hello, Eloise," I said, taking her hand. "I'm Amelia. And this is Grace."

"Call me, Slick," said Slick.

"Slick will be your buddy," I continued, "and I'll help out for a few days until Slick learns how we do things here. Do you have my voice now?"

She nodded.

"Speak to her," I whispered to Slick. "She needs to hear you."

"Ah, hi, Eloise. I'm Slick."

"Hi. You smoke."

Slick blushed. "Well, sometimes."

"I don't think so. I think lots." She sniffed the air around Slick. "It's all over your clothes. Just like my mom. She smokes, too." She took Slick's hand. "That's okay if you smoke. I'm glad you will play with me. Can I have a piece of your gum? It's cinnamon."

Slick looked amazed. "Yeah, I guess . . ."

"What were you doing when we came in, Eloise?" I asked while she maneuvered the gum out of its wrapper.

"Doing clay art. We are making our own faces."

"Why don't you show us?" I suggested.

She led us to her table and sat down.

"Hey, Amelia is here!" said one of the kids at the next table. "Hi, Amelia!"

"Hi there!"

"How'd he know it was you?" whispered Slick.

"Because Amelia always smells like lilacs," answered a little girl at our table.

"They don't miss much," mumbled Slick.

"Here! This is mine," said Eloise. "This is me. Only clay." She proudly held up her work.

It was a small face with a small nose and rounded cheeks. Masses of curly hair sat on top. There was a big smile holding the whole thing up.

Over the eyes were two flat strips of clay. Like blindfolds.

"See? I covered the eyes, because I don't use those. Mine don't work." Eloise took Slick's hand and ran it over the clay face. "Did I get me right, buddy? I mean, the rest of me?"

"Yes, you got it just right." Tears welled up in Slick's eyes. "It even looks a little bit like me," she said quietly. "It looks like me around the eyes."

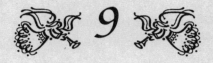

"*L*isten up, ladies!" yelled Miss Timmerman, the P.E. teacher, at the top of her drill sergeant lungs. "Due to the rain, everyone will report to the gymnasium for a game of indoor volleyball. All classes!"

"Oh, joy. Games in the gym*naus*ium," said my friend Luana. "But I'll look on the bright side, maybe this means we won't have to shower today."

"Don't bet on it!" I said with a laugh. "You know how she is about cleanliness . . ."

"It's next to godliness!" We finished in unison.

Lu and I changed into our ever-so-attractive gym suits, and reported to the gym.

"Hey, what's going on over there?" asked Lu, pointing to the front.

I craned my neck over a sea of girls to see Slick and Spooky being lectured by one of the gym teachers.

"Come on, Lu, let's get up a little closer," I suggested.

Luana and I wended our way to the front.

"Why should we have to dress?" asked Spooky. "It's raining. We should just get a day off. All sports should be called off on account of rain."

"Yeah," said Slick. She put her army boot up on the teacher's chair.

"Listen, it's hard enough being stuck inside. I can't let you two do what I won't let the others do," explained the teacher.

"So let us all wear our regular clothes." Slick crossed her arms and smirked. "Seems fair to me."

"This isn't about fair, it's about not disrupting everyone and everything. I want you two back in the locker room. Now!" The teacher was losing her patience. I could tell. She started to get that don't-press-me look on her face. My mom sometimes got the same look.

"They are cruisin' for a bruisin'," whispered Lu.

I nodded. Lu was right. But my question was, "Why?" I thought Slick was changing. She had been going to Bret Harte everyday for the past week, and she was doing well in the play. I was excited to think she had changed . . . but here she was. Up to her old Slick tricks.

"Amelia," whispered Lily, "change is frightening. Sometimes old tricks are the only tricks one knows."

I sighed and watched as Slick and Spooky got dragged away. They never did join the rest of us for volleyball.

And Slick didn't show up at play rehearsal, either.

That night, after dinner, I went for a walk with Dad while Mom and Kate worked on the angel costume.

The rain had stopped and the street lights were reflected in the pools of water. Drops of rain still clung and glistened on the trees.

"It's so pretty after it rains," I said.

"Yes, I remember rainy days. I used to go out with Aunt Jean and make little boats out of leaves and sticks, which we would sail in the gutter. I liked watching them get caught in the eddies, knowing that I could rescue them just before disaster, in the form of the sewer, would strike."

"How old were you then?"

"Probably four. That was the last year I could see things."

"That's when you got the retin . . . retin . . ."

"Retinoblastoma. A tumor in my left eye, which spread to my right one."

"Did it make you sad to be blind?"

"Not really. I was so young, and my parents never treated me like a victim. My blindness was simply something I had to deal with. I do recall missing the sight of my mother's face. But that's about it."

I closed my eyes and tried to imagine being blind, but it didn't work, because I knew, in my heart, that I was only pretending.

Dad stopped. "Listen," he whispered.

I listened. "I don't hear anything."

"I can hear the water running under the street in the sewers."

"Oh! Yes. Now I hear it. I had to listen hard, though."

"I'm in tune to sounds," he said as we continued around the neighborhood.

"Are you in tune to Slick Jamison at all?"

He smiled. "Ah, Slick. An enigma, wrapped in a puzzle."

"Huh?"

He laughed. "She's hard to figure."

"Don't I know it." I kicked a little rock along in front of me. "Today, at school, I saw her get in trouble again."

"That's too bad, but not too surprising."

"I was surprised. I thought she was doing so well at Bret Harte and, I don't know, I guess I thought she had turned over a new leaf."

"It's hard to turn over a new leaf when you're hanging from the same old tree."

"Yeah? Well, I wish she'd just drop off that old tree of trouble."

"She will. When she's good and ready. Or when a strong wind blows."

"I guess so." I breathed in the damp, cool air and watched a cloud cover the moon. "Dad, you said when you went blind you weren't sad."

"That's right."

85

"I know you're not scared of the dark now, but were you maybe a little scared back then?"

He seemed lost in thought for a few minutes before he responded. "Yes. I do remember feeling a little anxious because I knew I had to make my way in the dark. And as a child, I had always been just a little afraid of the dark." He stopped and put his arm around my shoulder. "I have a secret for you. I still have the night light that was in my nursery before I got sick."

"You do?"

"Yes. It reminds me that, once, a long time ago, I received comfort from the light. And I've always planned to put it in my child's room one day. To offer comfort when I can't be there."

"That's so sweet. It's just like you." I wiped the tears and the freshly falling rain off my face as we headed back home.

By the time we arrived, I had come up with one more plan in my quest to reach Slick. Maybe I could be the wind Dad had talked about.

When we walked in the door, we were greeted by an angel.

"Look at my costume, isn't it pretty?" Kate swirled around in front of us.

"Hey! That looks great! How on earth did you do it, Mom?" I stood back and gazed at Kate, in her white and silver, cloudy dress.

"Heaven must have helped me," said Mom, removing the pins from the hem. "It was easy after I cut down

86

that old white satin slip of mine. We found some wonderful, gauzy stuff in the fabric store, and the lady there was so helpful. She pretty much drew me a map.''

''Come here,'' said Dad. ''Let me get a look.''

Kate danced over on her toes, and he felt the dress. ''My, this is a dress fit for a princess!''

''Queen, my good man!'' corrected Kate.

''Oh, yes, excuse me, your highness.''

Kate giggled. ''I like that name; my highness sounds good.''

''Watch out there, your swellheadedness,'' I cautioned.

''Oh, yeah. Mommy reminded me already.'' She danced off into her room. ''It's hard to remember.''

We broke into laughter after her door closed.

''You know, this hadn't occurred to me, but what will we do if she actually wins?'' Mom came over and leaned on Dad.

''Prepare to be her slaves,'' I said.

''That's right,'' said Dad. ''Let's see, I'll polish her crown; Amelia, you hold up her train; and Fran will be in charge of all public appearances and tasteful make-up.''

''Well, we'll know soon enough. It's not long until the big 'Sunny' day,'' said Mom.

''That's right,'' I said. ''And *The Diary of Anne Frank* is only one week after that.''

''Good grief! We'll have two stars to contend with!'' said Dad.

"The house won't be big enough!" said Mom. "Their egos will take up all the space."

"We'll have to put on an addition to hold their big heads," Dad replied.

"You two are hilarious, and I am going to do my homework before I die of laughter." I shook my head at my weird parents and went to my room to hit the books.

The phone rang just as I opened my history book.

"Hi, Amelia Bedelia!"

"Hi, Richard. What's up?"

"My hopes."

"What for?"

"I have to ask you something."

"Okay. Ask away."

"Yeah, that's easy for you to say. I don't know who made the rule that guys have to do all the asking, anyway. It's not fair. All this equal rights stuff is great, but I think it really should extend to other areas, like asking people things."

"Richard, *what* are you talking about? So far, I don't have a clue."

"Okay, here's a clue: what's tall and thin, with braces, a mild case of zits, and a Valentine's dance to attend at a certain snooty school?"

I laughed. "Oh! You want me to go to a dance with you?"

"Ding! Ding! Ding! Ding! Ding! The lady wins an all-expense paid evening to the date of a lifetime. Whew! Glad that's over."

I cringed. "Oh, no."

"I do not like the sound of that. Sentences that start with 'oh, no' never bode well. Are you standing me up already? Before I even arrive?"

"Not on purpose. But there is no way I can go because the Miss Young Sunny California Beauty Pageant is that day, *all* day, and I can't miss it. I have to be there for Kate. I'm really sorry."

"Hey, wait. I think we're safe. Hold on while I get the announcement out of my pile."

The phone clattered to the floor and I heard him throwing things around his room. His cat, Cleopatra, yowled her annoyance at being disturbed.

"Okay, I'm back. It says here that the dance is on the Friday night before Valentine's Day!"

"Then I can definitely go."

"You're sure?"

"Positive."

"Great. That's a relief. One more thing . . ."

"What?"

"They're having a couple of ballroom dance lessons at my school. They think we should know how to do more than jiggle around and look awkward. You wanna go to them with me?"

"I would love that. It would be cool to dance for real, like they do in old movies. When are they?"

"First one is this Sunday. Every evening after that for a week or so. Until we stop clomping around like horses."

"Sure I can go. I'm home from play rehearsal by dinner."

"How is the play going?"

"Good, I think. It's starting to look and sound like a play now. My mom rented me the old movie of *Diary*, so I could see how it looked. And we're not as good as that, but we're not bad, either."

"How's everything with Slick Jamison?"

"It could be better. Just when I think we're friends, she makes it clear we're not. Oh, that reminds me, can you do me a favor after school tomorrow?"

"Sure. Name it. If it's free, I'll do it."

"It's free. It's at the library. I want you to look something up for me since I'm busy with rehearsal. I barely have time to brush my teeth lately."

"No problem. What do you need? The Flinkman is at your disposal."

I told him what I needed. And he said he would do it. I hoped so. Because my plan for Slick depended on it!

10

"Why do we have to go to the pageant so early?" Kate yawned and stared into her Cheerios.

"Because this stuff will take all day," I said with a yawn of my own.

Richard and I hadn't returned home from the Valentine's dance until midnight, and I was dance-lagged.

"I looked at the schedule," I continued sleepily, "and you have to be seen in a party dress, and in costume, and they have to interview you again, and you have to interact with the other girls so they can see if you're a spoiled brat."

Kate snorted and milk spurted out her nose.

When we were done laughing, she said, "I looked like a queen just then, for sure, didn't I?"

"You bet. Queen Snorty. How come you snorted?"

"Because you said they want to see if we're spoiled and I don't think they can tell that. It's too easy to fake being nice." She added more sugar to her bowl. "Like, there's this girl in my class, Donna, and she acts soooo sweet in front of the teacher, but she is a creepazoid out on the playground."

I laughed. "You're right, Kate. The pageant people can't tell much about you at all, except how you look on the outside."

She sighed and wiped her mouth. "That's fine with me. That's the part I like."

I swallowed my last bite and my disagreement. It was Kate's day. My opinion didn't count.

"Girls? You about done?" Mom stuck her electric-curlered head around the door. "We should be on the road in about twenty minutes."

"We'll be ready, Mom," I said. "Do you have all her stuff packed?"

"Daddy is in charge of keeping track of all that. I think he's packing the car right now." She came in and kissed Kate on the top of her head. "You remember something for me, Katykins."

"What, Mommy?"

"Beauty isn't on the outside. You remember that, and try to have fun."

"Okay, I will."

After Mom left Kate turned to me. "Melia, how come everybody tells me that pretty is on the inside?"

"Because it is." I cleared our dishes and put them into the dishwasher.

"That's not true." She turned around, straddled her chair, and watched me.

"Sure it is, it's just like I wrote about in *Swan Songs* . . ."

"Noooo," she interrupted. "That is how you all want it to be. Not how it really and truly is."

I started to argue with her, but I stopped. What could I say to the truth?

We climbed into the car right on time and got to listen to Kate sing "I Feel Pretty" all the way to the pageant.

The Marriott was packed with little princesses and their parents. We showed Kate's badge at the door and were directed to the ballroom by a man in a nice suit wearing a hat that said PAGEANT OFFICIAL.

"The gals in your age group will have the same color sunny badge!" he said jovially. "Mingle!"

"Wow!" said Kate as we entered the palatial ballroom. "This will take forever! Look at all these kids!"

"Remember, there are five different age groups," I warned. "So you have to wait while each group goes through the process."

"Gosh, there isn't much air in here," said Mom, fanning herself with a program. "It makes me woozy."

"Do you want to step into the lobby, dear?" asked Dad. "I'm sure I smelled an indoor garden and some coffee brewing somewhere."

"Yes, that sounds good. It looks as if we'll be here

for hours." She checked the program. "Amelia, would you mind staying with Kate? I see here that she isn't scheduled for anything for forty-five minutes."

"Sure. I don't mind. I kind of want to watch everybody."

"Thanks." She gave me a quick hug. "We'll catch up to you later."

"Stay together!" admonished Dad.

"Okay!" We watched them walk away, hand-in-hand.

"I'm sure glad we found him," said Kate.

"Yep. I guess having Mom around helped a little, too."

Kate giggled. "Oh, you know what I mean!"

"Yeah, I do."

We roamed around, me marveling at the sights, Kate checking out the competition.

"Boy," I said as we settled down in some folding chairs with a cup of complimentary orange juice, "some of these people go all out. Did you see some of the dresses and all that makeup?"

"I look kind of dull," she worried. "They all look like Barbie, and I look like Barbie's plain little sister, Skipit."

"Skipper," I corrected.

"Whatever." She fussed at the sash of her party dress. "I wish I could have worn more makeup and got a new dress."

"Makeup isn't so great." The soft, southern voice seemed to tap me on the shoulder.

We both turned to the girl on my left. She was like something out of a magazine. Her blonde hair was whipped into a froth of waves around her face. Blue eyes blinked at me from a fringed hood of carefully applied shadow and thick, black lashes. Her mouth was lined and filled in with pearl pink lipstick. It matched her silk outfit perfectly. In fact, everything about her was perfect. Not a hair out of place, not a fingernail out of alignment.

Kate and I stared dumbfounded.

"Hi, y'all," she said, extending her hand.

"Hi." I shook her hand and introduced us.

"Amelia and Kate. Those are real pretty names. My name is Arlee, which is not very pretty."

"Well, your face makes up for it!" Kate said.

Arlee laughed and smiled with her pearly, perfect whites. "Thank you, Kate."

"You're welcome." Kate stared at her. "I wish I could wear makeup like you."

"It might look good, but it is surely a piece of trouble. If I'm not having it put on, I'm having it scraped off." She sighed and half-smiled. "I can't touch my face or brush up against anything. Sometimes I forget and Ginny has a fit."

"Ginny?"

"My pageant assistant. She does my makeup and wardrobe and helps me with my talent. Ginny goes with me and my mother to all the pageants."

"You aren't from here?" I asked.

"Oh, no, Sugar! I'm from Alabama. This is just our

third pageant this month, is all! We go all over the place in our van. We don't miss many pageants.''

"You must really like them!" said Kate.

"I did at first." She looked around and lowered her voice. "But I am tired of them now. I have to whisper because my mother has a fit and falls in it if she hears me talk like that. She says it won't sound good if the judges hear me.''

"Why do you keep doing them?" Kate asked. "The pageants, I mean."

"I can't quit now. It means too much to my parents. They are so proud, they could burst. The day my picture was in our local paper, me with all the trophies, sashes, and crowns I have won, why I thought my father would die, he was so happy. He carried the clipping around for weeks, showing it to folks.''

Kate stared at her. "I guess you're kind of like his trophy, huh?''

Arlee ran a delicate finger over her arched eyebrow. "I never did think of it like that, but, yes, I guess so.''

"Arlee!" We all jumped and turned around.

A heavy-set lady with high blonde hair was standing behind us, tapping a pointed shoe. "Arlee Jean, didn't Ginny tell you not to sit in that thing? It's gonna wrinkle like an old apple, now you come on and circulate, the judges are watching!''

"Yes, Ma'am." Arlee stood and nodded in our direction. "Bye, y'all. Good luck.''

"Bye, Arlee," we chimed.

"I'm glad I don't *have* to be in the pageant," Kate said, "like Arlee does."

"Me, too."

"Does my dress look okay? Really?" Kate asked as she stood up.

"Sure. It looks good. Why?"

"I think I'll walk around and talk to some of the other girls. I have a feeling that's what I'm supposed to do right now."

"You want to go by yourself?"

"Uh-huh. The other girls are by themselves. You can see me from here. I'll be okay."

I nodded and watched as she held her head high and made her way through the crowds. She had more courage than I did!

Whenever I had the choice at social functions, between "wallflower" or "life of the party," I always planted myself in a back row, and practically grew roots!

It's funny how different sisters can be, I thought.

"Yes, it makes life more interesting, doesn't it?" Lily appeared next to me and continued, "It would be frightfully dull if people were the same."

"Yes. The girls here are *mucho* different from me. And it sure is interesting." As I watched, my mind wandered back to Arlee. "Lily, do you know anything about Arlee?"

"I do."

97

"Why doesn't her mother see that this life"—I swung my arm in an arc—"doesn't make Arlee happy anymore?"

"Because her mother is lost. Lost mothers can't guide their daughters."

"What do you mean?"

"Arlee's mother is like a lot of people, Amelia. Lost in their own lives, taking all the wrong roads. None of which will lead to happiness."

"It's hard, Lily. It's hard to know which road." I looked around the room at the anxiously smiling, painted faces. "These girls do look lost."

Lily nodded.

"How could they get on the right road? Do people have to be lost forever?"

"Of course not." Lily stood and rose above me, and the room. She spread her wings and said in a voice full of love, "All of you have a compass in your heart and a soul to light your way. Use them!"

For a moment, things got quiet. People looked around, as if they had heard something, but weren't quite sure. Then they shrugged and went back to what they had been doing.

Lily came down and hovered near me. "See? They don't trust what they hear in their hearts." She smiled. "But that's okay. Maybe they will. Someday."

"Maybe their hearts need hearing aids," I suggested.

"You're getting good at this, Amelia. I always knew you'd make a good Earthangel!"

I watched her fade. Her eyes always disappeared last. She winked at me.

"Who were you just talking to?" A pretty, color-coordinated girl sat down.

"Oh, um, nobody, really . . ." I stammered.

"Oh. Then, is this seat taken?"

"No. My little sister was sitting there before, but she's circulating."

"Good idea. I was too, but my feet are killing me. These heels aren't quite the right size, but they were just the right color."

I looked at them. "Yes, they match your outfit exactly. I didn't know they made violet shoes."

"They are nice, aren't they? I worked hard, shopping all day, to find these babies."

"My name is Amelia," I said.

"Hi. I'm Michelle."

"I guess you're in the pageant, huh?"

"Yes!"

"Do you like it?"

"No, I love it!" Michelle widened her eyes and checked her earrings. "I've been going to pageants since I was five. I think they're great, and a real learning experience. I meet lots of nice girls, and I learn how to be poised, and I get to travel."

It sounded like a little speech she had practiced.

"Have you won much?" I asked.

"Not to brag, but yes, I really have. The most I won was two thousand dollars last year at a national pageant.

This is just a regional, but it leads to a national. That's why we don't have to do a talent here.''

"Wow! I didn't know you could win so much."

"Oh, that's nothing. I've seen girls win as much as five thousand, and sometimes they even win a car. That's for the older girls, though.''

"How old are you?"

"Guess."

"Ah, sixteen? Seventeen?''

She laughed, but caught herself. "Oh, I shouldn't laugh big, it gives you wrinkles. But I couldn't believe how off you were on my age!''

"Are you older?"

"No, silly! I'm thirteen.''

I stared at the grown-up girl in front of me, and tried to see the thirteen-year-old underneath. But she was buried.

"How old are you?'' asked Michelle.

"Thirteen and a half. About.''

"Really? Gee, who'd ever guess we're the same age? You look so young.''

"I don't know,'' I said, with raised eyebrows. "Maybe this is what thirteen really looks like.''

"Not anymore it doesn't!''

I watched as she jumped up and ran over to talk to some man who was wearing a JUDGE sash.

I wondered how he could judge what he couldn't really see.

The pageant lasted all day and into the evening. The winners were announced at seven o'clock.

We stood with Kate when her age group was called.

I held her hand and felt the disappointment travel down her arm and up my own when her name wasn't called.

"Oh, no. I lost," she whispered.

Immediately, Dad was at her side. He picked her up. "Daddy's here."

He held her as she buried her disappointment in his shoulder.

We stood politely as all the winners were announced. Arlee won the biggest prize. I knew her parents would be thrilled.

"Let's go," said Mom. "I'm all pageanted out."

"Wait," I whispered. "It sounds like there's one more prize."

"And our final prize, a special one that we judges love, is the "Best Answer" award. We bestow this on the contestant who gives us the best answer to our final question during the personal interview." The chief judge fumbled through his sheaf of papers. "Ah, here it is. The question was 'If you could be anything or anyone for one day, what would it be?' And the winner is one of our younger girls."

Everyone stopped talking and looked up toward the stage.

"The little girl who won gave this answer, and I quote,

'Well, if I could be anything, I would be blind. My daddy is blind, and I would like to know how it is for him. And I think I could keep him company in the dark, for one day.' ''

We watched as the real winner of the beauty pageant went up and got her prize.

Then we took her out for pizza.

11

"So, Katerator, I hear you won the best prize at that old beauty roundup you went to." Richard threw her the basketball, and waited for her to shoot.

"I guess it was a good prize." She shot and missed. "I would have rather had a crown, though. A big one, with diamonds."

I rolled my eyes and retrieved the ball. "Well, I agree with Richard," I said as I shot and watched with surprise as the ball dropped through the hoop. "You won the prize that means something. It was more important than the one for being pretty."

"I guess. Everybody seems to say so, anyway." She shoved her hands in her pockets. "Flinkman, I'm tired. Can I go inside and visit with your mom?"

"Sure. I think she's making sandwiches and hot tea. She thinks we're crazy to be playing basketball in February! Even in California." He shot and missed.

Kate skipped to the backdoor and clanged inside. Cleopatra's tail grew fat, and she growled from her perch on the windowsill.

"It's all right, Cleo," I soothed. "You're safe up there. Don't be scared."

"Speaking of scared, how are you feeling? Any day-before-opening-night jitters?" Richard dribbled the ball, sort of, up the court, shot, and ran into the pole.

"Hey! Are you okay?" I hurried over and helped him up.

"I'm fine." He rubbed his nose. "Don't you know, Flinkmen bounce?"

I laughed. "Good thing. And I hope I bounce right through opening night. Actually, Slick goes on the first night. We drew straws and she won. Or lost, depending on your point of view."

"What do you do while she's on?"

"I'm backstage, helping with costumes and makeup. And that's what she'll do when I'm on."

"Well, my whole family is going to see it the night you're up there."

"Thanks. I hope I'm not too nervous."

We put the ball away and headed for the house.

"By the way, I wanted to thank you for getting that phone number for me, from the library," I said.

"No prob. They had phone books from all over the country."

"You're a lifesaver. I don't know what I'd have done without you!"

"Yeah. I kind of grow on you; like mold." He grinned and held the door open for me. "Are you gonna tell me what the number was for?"

"Nope. No can do." I smiled mysteriously and headed inside to the warm, friendly Flink kitchen.

He shrugged and headed for the pile of sandwiches.

That night at dinner, Mom wondered why we weren't very hungry.

"I like the stew, Mom," I protested, "but Mrs. Flink gave us club sandwiches at lunch and I'm still stuffed."

"Me, too," said Kate, pushing her stew away. "You know," she added innocently, "if we had that dog I've been asking for, then *he* could eat this old stew." She poked at it. "Especially these wrinkly peas."

"*No* dog," said Mom.

"I thought perhaps Amelia couldn't eat because of a nervous stomach," said Dad. "Actresses sometimes come down with a case of stage fright just before a big opening."

"I'm not nervous for me. Not yet anyway. I'm a little nervous for Slick." I stirred through my stew. "I really hope she does well on her opening night."

"That's nice of you," said Dad. "I think a success would be good for her."

"I think some new tee shirts would be good for her," said Kate.

He laughed. "Yes, I've heard about those shirts of hers. I think they are just the hard shell on a very soft egg."

"I hope so," I said.

And I had reason to hope. For my plan to work, Slick's softer side would have to show up. She sure better have one!

Opening night finally came, and it was insane!

Well, I guess the night wasn't insane, the performers were!

We arrived at the school late that afternoon, just after dinner.

"I hope you all took my advice and just ate soup," said Mr. Jacobs with a smile. "Or else we may have to deal with the after affects of too full stomachs while on stage."

"You mean belching and . . ."

"Yes, we all know what I mean," interrupted Mr. Jacobs. "I can always count on one of you boys to make these things crystal clear."

"I hope my lines are crystal clear," moaned Brian Siegel, who played Otto Frank. "I keep messing up in scene two where he has to get mad at Mr. Van Daan."

"Okay, somebody come over here in the corner and run through Brian's lines with him." Mr. Jacobs went around giving advice and offering help.

"How are Anne One and Anne Two doing?" he asked when he got to me and Slick.

"Not so good," replied Slick. "I don't know if I really want to do it now." She bit her nails and looked at the floor. "Maybe Amelia should just go on. I'll probably screw it up."

"Well, if you truly feel that way, and Amelia agrees . . . ?" He said this and shook his head at me at the same time.

I took the hint. "No way! I don't agree. I'm ready to go on tomorrow night. I can't do it tonight. Besides, Slick, you're just nervous. Everybody is."

"Thanks, pal," she said as she pushed past me and headed for the makeup table.

"She'll be okay," said Mr. Jacobs as he hurried off to check the costumes. "Don't leave her alone too long, though. Keep an eye on her for me."

I nodded and followed her.

"What the hell are you, my shadow, or what?" She glared at me in the mirror. "Get lost."

I cleared my throat. "I just wanted to tell you something."

"I don't need a pep talk."

"No. Nothing like that. It's just that Eloise told my dad, the other day at Bret Harte, that she wanted to be just like you when she grew up."

Slick blushed and busied herself with the makeup jars. "Yeah? Well, she's a sweet little kid. But, if she

107

could see me, her old buddy, she wouldn't think I was so great.''

What I did next surprised even me.

"You are so wrong. She can *see* you. In fact, she told me to give you this." I slipped my talisman from around my neck and handed it to her. "Eloise and some of the other kids made this . . . they made this for you and I know they want you to wear it tonight.''

Slick turned it over in her thin hands. " 'Wait for the day that maketh all things clear . . .' Hey, this is that thing they have over the door." She turned it over. "And there are some flowers engraved on the back.''

"Uh-huh. They know if you wear it, it will bring you good luck." I swallowed.

"Do you think so?"

"I know so. How could it not? I mean, it comes from their hearts. They love you.''

Her chin quivered and she put the talisman around her neck. "Man, I can't believe this. I never cry.''

"Never?" I met her eyes in the mirror.

"Hardly ever," she said. "Hey, thanks for bringing this to me. I'm sorry I bit your head off before.''

"It's okay. I know you didn't mean it.''

Just then, Brian Siegel flopped into the makeup chair. "Okay, Amelia, make me look like an old man!''

I laughed. "Oh, Brian, that won't be hard, you're already wrinkled!''

He laughed and hit me with the powder puff. Then Slick hit him with one of the wigs. Pretty soon, everyone

108

was in on it. Wigs flew and powder snowed.

"Knock it off!" yelled Mr. Jacobs. "We go on in just over an hour! Are you kids crazy?"

Slick giggled and whispered in my ear, "It took him long enough to figure out, didn't it?"

I nodded and smiled. It was the first time she had felt like my friend.

We settled down and were ready, willing, and anxious at fifteen minutes to curtain.

The junior high band screeched through a song out front to entertain the audience. Cast members paced and mumbled lines. Mr. Jacobs checked the curtains and lights and reminded the actors where to hit their marks.

I kept checking out front to see the people filing in. I was looking for someone in particular, although I didn't have any idea what he looked like.

Slick crept up behind me and peeked over my shoulder. I felt her stiffen.

"What?" I asked.

"I can't believe it," she whispered.

"What is it?" I turned and looked over my shoulder at her. I caught a glimpse of Lily, hovering just behind Slick.

"See that tall, thin guy, with the dark hair? Holding that little kid?"

"Where?"

"There. In the second row."

"Yeah. I see them now. Hey, he's with your grand-mother . . ." My hopes flew to the rafters.

"That's because he's my father."

I let the curtain drop. "Wow, Slick, that is so neat. He came all this way just to see you. Somebody, I mean, your grandma, must have called him."

"I can't believe it. I made her promise she wouldn't tell him." She paced back and forth in the small space. "I mean, the last thing I told him in Oregon was that I hated him, and I never wanted to see him again."

"I guess your family knew you didn't mean it," I said.

"Man, now I am really nervous. I don't want to disappoint him. He came all this way and everything. What if I blow it?"

"You won't."

She felt for the talisman underneath her costume.

Mr. Jacobs called for quiet backstage. "Remember kids, just do your best. The audience won't know if you blow a line. They don't have scripts. Be respectful of the words you are saying. Don't ever forget that these people lived this story. We are here to honor them."

The music died out. And the play came to life.

And I knew, as I watched alone from the wings, that Slick had come to life, too.

Lily put a hand on my shoulder and whispered, "Very well done, my dear."

"Thanks." I bit my lower lip. "I'll miss my talisman, though."

"I know. But you gave so much more than you lost."

I wiped my face and smiled. "It's hard being good, Lily. Isn't it?"

Her wings rose in the air around us and covered me in an embrace. "Yes, it is. But every time you do something good, the darkness in the world is pierced with light. And at that instant, some evil, somewhere, is stopped in its tracks. And the angels sing. Listen . . ."

And, finally, I heard.

It was the day things became a little more clear.

12

"Oh, sorry!" I apologized to the person I had run into on the steps outside Bret Harte.

"Hey, don't you even recognize me?"

I shaded my eyes and looked up. "Slick! No, I didn't," I sputtered, "but I wasn't really paying attention . . ."

She smiled. "It's okay. I was just giving you a hard time, for old time's sake."

I laughed. "Yeah, well, without your tee shirt, I could hardly recognize you."

She smiled and leaned against the railing. "I guess you heard why I haven't been around."

"My dad told me. I think it's great that you and your grandma are going to move to Oregon."

"Me, too. I think maybe I'll turn over a new leaf. It'll be easier where nobody knows me."

"Much easier. I hope you'll write to me. I love to get letters, and I really will answer."

"Fine with me. Just be sure you address them to Grace Jamison." She grinned. "That's the name of my new leaf."

"Pretty name."

"Listen," she leaned forward. "I just found out back in there"—she gestured into the school—"that this talisman is really yours." She slipped it off.

"No, no. It's not really mine. See, it's meant to be spread around. You know, passed from person to person. I gave it to another friend before you, and when she was done, she gave it back."

"How will I know who to give it to?"

"You'll know, Sl—Grace. You'll know when you don't need it anymore, and then you'll see someone who does. Believe me."

"If you say so." She shrugged and put it back around her neck. "Well, I guess I better go, and I guess I should thank you or something." She extended her hand awkwardly.

I ignored it and gave her a hug.

She wiped the tears from her clean face. I noticed her hair dye was fading, and her nose ring was gone.

I waved until I couldn't see her anymore.

"Geez," I marveled aloud. She looked like a whole different girl.

Lily appeared and held my hand. "Yes, and it is because that which is loved, reveals its loveliness."

I thought about that all afternoon.

That night after dinner Kate and I hurried through the dishes.

"Why do you think Mommy and Daddy want to talk to us?" Kate asked as she carefully lined the plates up in the dishwasher.

"I don't know. Have you done anything bad lately?"

"*Me*? I'm never bad."

I looked at her.

"I'm interesting."

I laughed. "Yeah, right."

We finished and joined our parents in the living room.

"Okay, what did we do?" I asked.

"Nothing," said Mom. "We just want to watch a movie together tonight."

"Oh, is that all!" said Kate. "You always like to watch old movies, how come you made it into a big deal?"

"This movie is a big deal," said Dad.

"What is it? *Gone With the Wind*?" I kicked off my shoes, settled onto the couch, and pulled my legs up under me.

"No. It's called, *Yours, Mine, and Ours*." Mom waited, like we should be thrilled or something.

"I guess they don't know what it's about," said Dad.

"Then tell us already!" said Kate.

Mom sat down on Dad's lap and explained. "Let's see, it's about this man and woman who fall in love and get married. Only they already have some kids. So when the mother gets pregnant . . ."

I screamed and jumped up. "We're having a baby! We're having a baby!"

"What?" yelled Kate. "I wanted a puppy!"

We all laughed and talked at once.

A baby. What a gift.

Later that night I found Dad in his den, using his Braille measuring tape.

"Will this be the nursery?" I asked.

"Yes, it's light and airy. And just the right size. Maybe we'll paint it before the baby comes."

"I'll help."

"I thought so." He lifted something out of a box. "Maybe you'll help me with this, too."

"What is it?"

"It's the night-light I told you about."

"Oh," I whispered, "the one from your room . . ." I took it out of his hands. "It's so sweet, Dad."

He smiled. "Can you make out the little picture on the front? It hasn't faded?"

"No fading. The picture is still there. And very clear."

I held it up and smiled at the angel, still guarding the light.

That night I put on my robe and crept out to the tiki. I made my wish and stared up at the stars.

"Did you wish for a boy or a girl?" asked Lily.

"Neither. I wished for Mom and the baby to be okay."

"They will be."

"Good." I saw a falling star streak through the sky. "Look! How pretty!"

"Another angel being sent down. There is much work to be done." Lily crossed her arms and gazed into the starry, starry night.

"I hope you angels don't give up on us," I said quietly.

"We won't. Never."

"That's good," I said. "Because I'm just getting the hang of this Earthangel stuff."

"And we're just getting started!" Lily smiled and faded away.

As I looked upward, three falling stars shot through the sky.

"Welcome," I whispered.

From out of the Shadows...
Stories Filled with Mystery
and Suspense by

MARY DOWNING HAHN

TIME FOR ANDREW
72469-3/$3.99 US/$4.99 Can

DAPHNE'S BOOK
72355-7/$3.99 US/$4.99 Can

THE TIME OF THE WITCH
71116-8/ $3.99 US/ $4.99 Can

STEPPING ON THE CRACKS
71900-2/ $3.99 US/ $4.99 Can

THE DEAD MAN IN INDIAN CREEK
71362-4/ $3.99 US/ $4.99 Can

THE DOLL IN THE GARDEN
70865-5/ $4.50 US/ $6.50 Can

FOLLOWING THE MYSTERY MAN
70677-6/ $3.99 US/ $4.99 Can

TALLAHASSEE HIGGINS
70500-1/ $3.99 US/ $4.99 Can

WAIT TILL HELEN COMES
70442-0/ $3.99 US/ $5.50 Can

THE SPANISH KIDNAPPING DISASTER
71712-3/ $3.99 US/ $4.99 Can

THE JELLYFISH SEASON
71635-6/ $3.50 US/ $4.25 Can

THE SARA SUMMER
72354-9/ $3.99 US/ $4.99 Can

Stories of Adventure From
THEODORE TAYLOR
Bestselling Author of THE CAY

THE OUTER BANKS TRILOGY

STRANGER FROM THE SEA: TEETONCEY
71024-2/$3.99 US/$4.99 Can
Ben O'Neal spotted a body on the sand—a girl of about ten or eleven; almost his own age—half drowned, more dead than alive. The tiny stranger he named Teetoncey would change everything about the way Ben felt about himself.

BOX OF TREASURES: TEETONCEY AND BEN O'NEAL
71025-0/$3.99 US/$4.99 Can
Teetoncey had not spoken a word in the month she had lived with Ben and his mother. But then the silence ends and Teetoncey reveals a secret about herself and the *Malta Empress* that will change their lives forever.

INTO THE WIND: THE ODYSSEY OF BEN O'NEAL
71026-9/$3.99 US/$4.99 Can
At thirteen, Ben O'Neal is about to begin his lifelong dream—to go to sea. But before Ben sails, he receives an urgent message from Teetoncey, saying she's in trouble.